This book is for my children, Caroline and Christopher, and for their horses: Hombre, who's too hot to handle, Minnie, who has her moments, but most of all for Sam. He is the good, honest, dependable horse that should be everyone's first pony, and he is truly as still. May I wish you all a Sam in your lives. He won't be the best horse you ever ride, nor the most exciting, but he is the one you will remember with love.

COTTESMORE SCHOOL

1894   1994

1.S. Improvement
                    Prize.

Molly Tregear.

Summer 1994.

CALL ME BRAVE

Elizabeth Walker

Piper Original
PAN MACMILLAN
CHILDREN'S BOOKS

First published 1993 by Pan Macmillan Children's Books

a division of Pan Macmillan Publishers Limited
Cavaye Place London SW10 9PG
and Basingstoke

Associated companies throughout the world

ISBN 0-330-32714-3

Copyright © 1993 Elizabeth Walker

The right of Elizabeth Walker to be identified as the
author of this work has been asserted by her in accordance
with the Copyright, Designs and Patents Act 1988.

All rights reserved. No reproduction, copy or transmission
of this publication may be made without written permission.
No paragraph of this publication may be reproduced, copied or
transmitted save with written permission or in accordance with
the provisions of the Copyright Act 1956 (as amended). Any
person who does any unauthorised act in relation to
this publication may be liable to criminal prosecution
and civil claims for damages.

1 3 5 7 9 8 6 4 2

A CIP catalogue record for this book is available from
the British Library

Phototypeset by Intype, London

Printed and bound in Great Britain by
Cox & Wyman Ltd, Reading, Berkshire

This book is sold subject to the condition that it shall not,
by way of trade or otherwise, be lent, re-sold, hired out,
or otherwise circulated without the publisher's prior consent
in any form of binding or cover other than that in which
it is published and without a similar condition including this
condition being imposed on the subsequent purchaser

Chapter One

There wasn't anything anyone could do. They stood and watched, open mouthed, as the horse thundered down the field in a headlong gallop, threatening to overbalance at every stride. Susie seemed to be doing nothing except pull the reins in a stiff line from the horse's mouth to her hand, but the horse never faltered. The girl's face was set in a white mask of terror.

'They'll crash into the wall!' gasped someone, but they didn't. The horse saw the obstacle, gathered himself and jumped. Susie's body whipped back, then forward, and kept on going. She hit the ground with a hard, dead thud.

She hurt all over. Her head ached, her shoulder throbbed and her teeth would not stop chattering. But her mother's silence was worse. Mrs Diamond stood at the sink, peeling vegetables in a silence as thick as a blanket, a heavy, choking cover. Finally, Susie could bear it no longer.

'I'm sorry, Mum,' she said.

Mrs Diamond turned. 'Sorry. You're sorry. You realize you lost me a sale? No one will buy that horse after your exhibition. How many times have I told you that it does no good at all to sit like a stone and haul on his mouth? You never listen to a word I say. I might as well talk to myself.'

'He's too strong. I couldn't hold him.'

'You didn't try, you mean.'

Mrs Diamond moved to the fridge, her stiff leg dragging awkwardly. Her face was drawn, with weariness and disappointment. She seemed very pale, and even her lovely red hair looked lank and unhappy.

Susie, near to tears, said, 'I couldn't help it, Mum. Really.'

Her mother moved clumsily round and looked at her. She stood with a pound of margarine in her hand, the cheap sort that was all they could afford, and she was so disappointed. 'Oh, Susie, I am so tired of the way you always make such a mess of things. We really needed that sale. For once, just for once, couldn't you try to do it right?'

Susie's eyes flooded with tears. She got up and ran into the yard.

She sat in the barn and cried into the fur of one of the cats, the ginger one that always kept her company while she groomed. It was a big, warm animal, so happy to be cuddled that it purred even when she soaked its fur with tears. After a while she got up and went to look at the horse. Diamond Bright.

They had given him the name when he was foaled, four years before. He was out of Mrs Diamond's old event mare, a spirited chestnut that Mrs Diamond couldn't bear to sell, even when her accident meant she could ride no more. They had saved and saved to send the mare to a really good stallion, and they had chosen Bright Morning, coal black and beautiful. But even he was not as beautiful as the foal. Red chestnut with black streaks in mane and tail, his huge eyes luminous with interest and excitement, Diamond Bright pricked his ears and whickered as Susie came near.

She put her arms around his neck and said, 'Diamond, how could you? I so wanted you to behave.'

The horse snorted and pulled away. He never wanted to be petted. He was tough and clever, always looking for the chance to have fun and get his own way. He walked to his manger and blew into it, then lifted his neat head and stared at Susie expectantly.

'You want me when it's feed time, don't you?' she said crossly. 'That's all I'm good for. Feeding, and grooming, and tack cleaning, and *always* mucking out! If it wasn't for me you'd starve and live in filth, but do you care? No. You're a horrible horse – I hate you!'

As she stormed away across the yard he came to the door and called after her. Susie stopped, shoulders drooping. There were ten horses in the yard and they all had to be fed, even Diamond Bright. She might as well get on with it.

The work seemed very hard that night, stiff and bruised as she was. She tried not to think of how much there was to do, instead moving mechanically from box to box, letting her thoughts drift. Things had been so different when her father was alive.

They had taken just a few liveries then, and employed a girl to help, and her mother gave lessons to event riders who wanted to improve. She had time for Susie then.

But when Daddy died it turned out there wasn't any money saved and hardly any pension, so Mrs Diamond had sacked the girl and taken more liveries and given more lessons. But, try as they might, things had gone down and down. Now they were poor as church mice.

'I'd rather be a church mouse,' said Susie out loud. 'They don't have to lug huge sacks and bales. They don't have to get up at dawn and work when it's freezing and get thrown off beastly horses that never do what you want. A church mouse has nothing to do but frighten old ladies in the hymns.'

Out of the evening gloom, a voice said, ''Scuse me.'

Susie screamed.

The voice said, 'Jesus! You are a mouse, and that's a fact!'

A figure appeared, small, scruffy, coming out of the dark into the lighted yard. It was a young lad.

Susie said, 'You sneaked up on me! You meant to frighten me, didn't you?'

'Talking to yourself, you was,' said the boy.

He was so short he might have been quite young, but was probably sixteen or so. He had small, bright eyes in a pale, lumpy face, and black hair that needed cutting. He wore jeans and old trainers, and a stained donkey jacket, the sort builders wear. He had a red scarf tied loosely around his neck.

Susie got on with her work: haynet, water bucket, feed; haynet, water bucket, feed. Her fall had made her stiff and slow, and it was awkward, the boy watching all the time. Why didn't he say why he was there? Perhaps he was a friend of one of the liveries, in which case he would ask her questions. But he just stood, watching her.

'Look,' said Susie suddenly, turning on him. 'Do you want something?'

He nodded. 'Job.'

'We don't want anyone.'

'No harm in asking, is there? You in charge?'

Susie shook her head.

'Well then. Who do I ask?'

'My – my mother. But she doesn't want anyone, honest. I do all the work around here.'

'Is that right?'

He looked about him at the yard, and just from his face Susie could tell he was criticizing. Straw was blowing, the muck heap was a mess and all the doors needed a coat of paint. She felt ashamed of the place, and ashamed of being poor. It wasn't her fault, she wanted to shout. It wasn't up to her to make everything right! Sometimes she even got a lift home from school in the lunch-hour, to try and catch up, and sometimes she didn't bother to go back. Her last report had been terrible.

The boy said, 'Where do I find your mum, then? To ask.'

Susie tossed back her hair. 'You don't. I'll ask for you.'

He was making her feel angry. She always felt like that when people criticized her, and the way he stood there, looking, was infuriating. She walked to the house and flung into the kitchen, leaving the boy in the yard outside.

Mrs Diamond was sitting at the table, doing accounts. She glanced up as Susie came in. 'Finished? Supper's almost ready.'

'There's someone here,' said Susie.

'Someone? A customer? Why don't you bring them in?'

'He wants a job. In the stables. A boy.'

Her mother gave an exasperated sigh, and looked at her daughter as if she was an idiot. 'Susie, you know we can't afford to employ anyone! We haven't a single spare penny. Tell him to go away.'

Susie had known she would say that. It was only sensible. But all at once she knew she didn't want to go and tell the boy that they didn't need help. Because they did.

She stood on one leg, unhappily. It wasn't easy to talk to her mother. Since Dad died she might fly into a rage, or cry, or anything, if Susie said the slightest thing. She took a deep breath. 'Mum, we've got to have help. I'm getting in trouble at school and it's going to be worse if I don't do well in the exams. I can't pass *and* see to the horses.'

'But you get time to do your homework, don't you? I always make sure you've time.'

Susie nodded dumbly. The trouble was, she was so tired she fell asleep over her books. In class too, her thoughts kept drifting to the horses. There was too much to think about, too much to do!

'Anyway,' went on her mother, 'I thought you wanted to work with horses? This is invaluable training, you must see that.'

'I – I've changed my mind.'

Her mother's eyes widened. 'You've what? Susie, you've always wanted a career with horses!'

'No, I haven't,' said Susie desperately. 'You've wanted it for me. I hate the work and I hate the horses and most of all I hate Diamond Bright!'

Her mother struggled for patience. 'You're just going through a bad patch,' she said soothingly. 'Your fall today upset you. I knew you should have got straight back on. You used to be a wonderful rider, you used to love the horses! Don't you remember when you and Daddy used to argue over who could ride best? You'll feel better after a rest. It's been a long, hard winter and we're both tired. I know I've been short with you lately, but if we can just build the business up then we can run it together, when you leave school. I thought you wanted that.'

Susie hung her head. 'I want to do well in my exams,' she muttered.

'Why? What else is it that you want to do?'

Susie said nothing. She didn't know what she might want, she only knew that without her exams it would be this, for ever and ever.

Mrs Diamond dragged herself to her feet. The fine, freckled skin over her nose was taut with anger. 'Honestly, Susie, can't you for once put yourself in my shoes? What am I to do? We can hardly make ends meet as it is and you want me to hire people and spend money. Don't you realize how difficult it is for me? If we'd sold Diamond Bright today then things might have been different, but you put paid to that. You always let me down!'

Her mother was near to tears. It was always like this when Susie tried to talk. Her mother didn't mean the things she said but they hurt just the same. If only her father was still alive. He used to say Susie's mother was angry at herself and her crippled leg, and not Susie at all. It was just that she wanted Susie to do all the things that she knew she could never do again. She had been a brilliant rider, Dad used to say. It was very hard for her to lose all that. Suddenly Susie could almost see him, leaning back in his armchair with the paper, looking over his glasses, making the arguments seem the silly things they were. For a second she almost thought she could hear his voice. It settled her.

'Perhaps the boy can ride,' said Susie. 'He might show the horses. We might sell one then.'

Mrs Diamond turned her head. 'Does he look as if he can ride?'

Susie said, 'Yes.'

She went to the door and called, 'Boy! Can you come in?'

He came, reluctantly. They had kept him waiting an age.

'Do you have a name?' she asked.

He nodded. 'Black. Reuben Black.'

'Oh. I'm Susie Diamond, and this is my mother, Mrs Diamond. Reuben Black,' she repeated.

He stood in front of the table, unhappy and out of place.

'Susie says you can ride,' Mrs Diamond began.

'Aye.'

'And you're experienced in stable work?'

'Aye.'

Mrs Diamond sighed, and ran a hand through her hair. 'I don't really want anyone at all,' she said. 'But I suppose, if you're here we could take you on for a few weeks. I'll need references, of course. I'll write to the people you've worked for. Susie, find a piece of paper, he can give me their names and addresses.'

Susie brought pen and paper, but she stood looking at the boy. His face was closed and sullen. 'Perhaps this is your first job?' she said.

The boy looked up and met her eye. He nodded, vigorously.

'Oh. Oh, I see,' said Mrs Diamond. 'In that case we can forget the references. And we won't be able to pay you much at all, since you will really be learning.'

'I know about horses,' said the boy. 'Horse dealers, we are. Horses are me life.'

'That we shall have to see,' said Mrs Diamond.

The formalities over, they expected him to leave. Instead, his sharp button eyes looked from one to the other. 'Got somewhere for me to sleep, have you?' he said.

'Sleep? I didn't realize you wanted to live in.'

'There's always the stable flat,' said Susie, quickly.

It was where the girl used to live when they could afford outside help.

'It's a bit of a mess,' said Mrs Diamond. 'No one's lived in it for ages.'

'Don't mind that,' said the boy, and for the first time he sounded hopeful, and pleased.

Susie took him to the old brick stable. The hayloft had been made into two rooms, one with a bed and a cooker, the other with a lavatory and bath. There were mouse droppings on the floor and an old sixties poster was pinned up on the wall, showing a girl with beehive hair and flares.

'Bet your mum looked like that once,' said Reuben.

'Yes.' It didn't seem very likely. It was hard to remember a time when her mother had laughed and had fun. Susie looked around at the bare floor and the dusty bed. 'Is this really all right? I can bring you some blankets and things. And some supper.'

He looked small and cold and anxious. 'That's good. Great.'

He was looking at the poster on the wall. He tilted his head, turning the words 'Swinging Sixties' upside down, as if they were a puzzle. And he'd flinched the moment Susie's mother mentioned writing.

'You can't read, can you?'

Dull red colour flushed his face. 'Bother you, do it?' he said gruffly.

She shrugged. 'No. I won't tell if you don't want.'

He nodded, as if that was settled.

She ate her supper in the kitchen, all the time

thinking of the boy eating his in the dirty, mouse-ridden loft. This could be a terrible mistake. He might not know anything about horses.

'Susie.'

She looked up. Her mother was watching her intently.

'Susie, I'm sorry about today. All the things I said. I was just so upset and disappointed. Do you hurt anywhere?'

'No,' Susie lied.

'I don't mean to be cruel,' said her mother. 'But I really need you to help, and lately you've been so difficult. You know I can't work the horses myself, but when I tell you what to do with them it's as if you don't listen. What is it, Susie?'

The girl ducked her head. She was tired and she ached all over and there was no way she could explain. Mrs Diamond sighed, and began to clear the plates. Susie was being difficult again. She didn't understand her daughter at all nowadays.

Chapter Two

The yard was alive before seven the next morning. Susie woke to the sound of taps and buckets, and looked out to see the boy working in the yellow glare of the floodlights. She opened her window and leaned out.

'You're early. Do you want me to help?'

He glanced up at her. 'Nope.'

'What about the feeds? You can't read the chart.'

'Get what they look like. Best way. I'll make out.'

She shut her window and retreated gratefully to bed. What did he mean, 'Get what they look like?' Suppose he poisoned the liveries, or didn't soak the sugar beet, or gave Diamond a whole scoop of oats and made him even more crazy than he was already? If he did that was just too bad, she thought, snuggling down for her longest lie-in for months. Bliss.

She woke to find her mother standing over her. 'Susie, you're going to be late for school!'

'What?' She shot out of bed. Half past eight.

'You've missed the bus, I'll have to drive you. I don't know how we overslept, we've done nothing in the yard. I've a lesson at nine and I'll never get straight!'

But as they rushed into the yard, Susie with her ginger hair all on end, her mother fighting to get an arm in her coat, they stopped dead. Everything was brushed and tidy. All the horses looked contentedly out over their doors, even Moonraker, a weaver who swung endlessly from side to side all day if he could manage. Today his haynet was hung in the doorway and his nervous swinging was halted.

'Well,' said Mrs Diamond. 'What a picture.'

Reuben looked out over a box door. 'Horse here got thrush. Can't find stuff.'

'I keep the medicines in the house,' said Mrs Diamond.

'Best give them here. No need to be asking you every time horse needs sommat.' Mrs Diamond blinked. But the boy went on. 'Don't like that big bay.'

'Major? Yes, I should have warned you — he kicks and bites.'

'Won't when I've done with him. Cheeky _____.'

Mrs Diamond went bright pink. She and Susie hurried to the car.

'I'll have to ask him not to swear,' said Mrs Diamond as they drove to school. 'He's a gypsy, of course. I wonder if he'll steal?'

'Of course he won't,' said Susie. 'I mean — will he?'

'You never can tell,' said her mother. 'But we haven't much to steal. He seems an excellent worker, even if he does seem to think he's in charge!'

They looked at each other and grinned. It was a new day and yesterday's squabbles were forgotten. Susie wished they didn't argue so much. Her father used to say it was because they were so alike, both as hot-tempered and determined as each other. Neither of them ever knew when to back down.

They drew up at the school. 'Don't be late tonight,' said Mrs Diamond. 'I need you to exercise Major, he hasn't been out in days.'

Susie felt her heart sink. 'Couldn't you lunge him or something? I hate Major.'

'He needs some proper schooling. Mr Barnstaple's bound to want to ride on Saturday and you know how hopeless he is at telling Major off. If the horse gets any worse he might decide to sell him. We can't afford to lose the money, so you've got to ride Major. Be a good girl, Susie.'

All day, whenever her thoughts strayed from her lessons, Susie thought about Major. He was a big, nasty horse, all on his forehand, and an hour's work on him left her with legs like spaghetti and arms like string. He pulled and he yawed, tried to bang her knees on gates and threw his head and tried to hit her in the face. She hated riding him.

But the trouble with liveries was that you never got to ride the nice horses. The owners did that. All you got were the ones with problems, the slugs and the bolters, the rearers and the sticky jumpers. It was your job to make sure that come Saturday someone else had a nice ride, profiting from all your hard work. She didn't used to mind as much as she did now. There had been a time when she enjoyed riding, but somehow, not any more.

Glumly, she got on the school bus at the end of the day.

'Come over to my house,' said Ellen, her best friend. 'We can do our homework together.'

'Can't. Got to ride Major,' said Susie.

Naomi Fisher, who was in their form, said, 'Oh, hark at her! Brilliant Susie Diamond, showing the horse world how it's done. What a pity you never seem to have any money.'

'We've got plenty of money,' said Susie stiffly, and Naomi shrieked with laughter.

'Then why does your mother drive that dreadful car? I saw it this morning, more rust than anything else. Pathetic, that's what I call it.'

Susie blushed a fiery red.

Ellen glared at Naomi. 'You're just jealous because Susie rides so much better than you. Didn't she school your pony when you couldn't? Didn't she?'

Naomi yawned, pretending to be bored. 'Oh, that. So long ago I'd almost forgotten.'

'Susie's a brilliant rider,' declared Ellen.

Susie went redder still. 'I'm not,' she muttered. 'Really I'm not.'

'Oh, come off it!' Oliver, the school heart-throb, and two years older, joined in. 'I bet you'll be famous one day. Susie the Centaur.'

'What's a centaur?' asked Ellen.

Oliver groaned. 'Why are girls always so thick?'

When Susie got home she asked her mother what a centaur was.

'A creature from mythology,' said Mrs Diamond. 'Half man, half horse. Why?'

'Someone at school said I must be one.'

'You?' Mrs Diamond laughed. 'Not after your performance on Diamond Bright! But Reuben might be. You're right, Susie, he can ride. I put him up on Diamond this afternoon and he's not bad. No style, of course, arms and legs everywhere, but I can teach him. He has real natural talent.'

Susie changed into her old exercise jodhpurs, picked up her crash hat and went out into the yard. Reuben was sitting by the trough, fishing bits one by one out of the water and polishing them.

'Right mess this lot's in,' he said. 'Right mess.'

'It's not my fault,' snapped Susie.

'Never said it were.'

She relaxed a little. She didn't have to fight everybody, Reuben included. 'We've been letting things get on top of us lately,' she muttered. 'I think we were both starting to lose heart.'

'Thought as much. Good thing I came, then.'

'Yes.'

She watched him for a moment. He had small, strong hands with nails dirty from work. The water in the trough was ice cold but he hardly seemed to notice, and Susie said, 'My mother said you were a gypsy.'

He stopped then, and looked up at her. His eyes were like black buttons, and they stared right into her. 'We don't like that name,' he said. 'Travellers, we are. But we don't travel no more. Council house we got. No horses, no hens, and the neighbours writing dirty words on the door that we can't read.'

'Is that why you're here? Because you didn't like it?'

'I don't tell you what I like and what I don't.'

'No.'

'Nothing says we can't still travel, if we wants. Nothing to keep me here if I don't want to stay.'

'No. Sorry.'

She had upset him. She went to saddle Major, puffing under the weight of Mr Barnstaple's old military saddle, still with the brass plate stamped with a number. It had belonged to his father, but Mr Barnstaple liked to imagine himself as a great general of old, going into battle on his charger. It was a pity Major was so horrid and Mr Barnstaple couldn't ride.

The horse tried to whip round and bite her as she did up his girth, but Susie hit him on the neck and yelled, 'Grrrrrr!' He tried to back her into the wall and kick her too, but she slipped away and got to his head, and he grumbled and rolled his eyes. She tightened the strap of her crash hat. Why, oh why did she have to do this?

She took him in the field and began steady circles at walk and trot. The horse was lazy and wouldn't work, but if she hit him he would buck. A figure came and leaned on the gate and for a horrible moment she thought it was her mother. It wasn't. It was Reuben.

'Give him a belt,' he shouted.

'No.'
'Go on.'
'No!'

She rode on, trying to ignore her audience. But when she asked Major to canter the horse bucked anyway, and each time she asked the question he did it again. If he did this with Mr Barnstaple it would be a disaster, she thought, but she dared not hit the horse. She just dared not.

A clod of earth flew across the field and landed fair and square on the horse's backside. Major shot into a canter, and did two energetic circuits, snorting in surprise. Reuben squealed with laughter.

'Don't do that!' yelled Susie. 'I could have been hurt!'

'That horse don't have no respect,' shouted Reuben. 'He's taking advantage. Go on like that and he'll end up cat food!'

Susie felt hot with anger. She turned Major and rode over to the gate, then slipped from the saddle. 'You try,' she said. 'You can borrow my hat.'

He took the hat with a grin that told her he had wanted to ride Major all along. She hoped he got thrown.

But Reuben leaped easily into the saddle. He lifted the whip and gave Major two sharp cuts, and Susie jumped back, expecting at any moment to see the horse charging off. Instead he put his head down, accepted his bit and decided to work.

After ten minutes Susie went in to do her homework. It hardly mattered that she was riding so badly, she told herself, closing the window and turning her back on the yard. She didn't like horses any more. She had once, when she was younger, but nowadays she disliked them. As Ellen said, and even Naomi Fisher, horses were boring. There were lots more interesting things to do than ride. Yes, Susie decided, if someone else would do the work then she was more than happy.

But somehow, when Reuben brought Major back into the yard, covered in honest sweat and unusually meek and well behaved, she found herself wandering out to meet them.

'How was he?'

'Not bad. Needs some bossing, that's all.'

'Are you saying I should have bossed him?'

'You know that well enough. Can't, that's all.'

'Of course I could!'

'Then why don't you?'

She opened her mouth and closed it again. Reuben glanced at her. 'I'll tell you why,' he said. 'You're scared.'

Susie opened her mouth to deny it, but no words came out. And the boy didn't seem to expect any. He turned his back and started work on the horse, taking the saddle off and wisping the sweat from Major's steaming flanks.

'Don't tell my mother,' said Susie.

Reuben said, 'Anyone can see. You can't boss a horse. Can't do nothing with 'em. You're scared and you can't.'

Susie felt like crying, and for a moment she hated

the boy, because he knew. She didn't want anyone to know. 'I've been riding for years,' she said lamely. 'Since before I could walk. It's just – it's just—'

'It happens,' said Reuben. He didn't want her to explain, and anyway, she didn't know if she could.

It had been coming for a long time now. At the beginning it had been no more than a shiver of nerves, and soon went away. But somehow it had got worse and worse. Yesterday, when her mother told her to get up on Diamond, her legs had felt too weak to keep her up. Everything had seemed quiet and far away, as if she was in a dream, with nothing real. A second later, on the horse, she had felt scared enough to be sick.

Her mother had never been scared. On the day of her accident, riding a gelding known to be wild, she hadn't flinched. Susie had been very small, she could only just remember her mother smiling and waving to her, the horse bucking and pulling, desperate to be off. What she remembered far more clearly was her mother's dark red hair, redder than Susie's, spread out on the mud by the fence, and her leg all twisted underneath her. She remembered that all right.

Even now, with her stiff and painful leg, her mother had courage. Mrs Diamond would sometimes have them lift her on a horse and she would try and ride. But all it did was put her in bed for two days, so there really wasn't any point.

Susie felt so useless. Even Mr Barnstaple rode Major, and the thought of riding him had ruined Susie's whole day. She felt scared, and ashamed, and miserable.

Reuben picked up a sponge and rinsed Major's mouth with clean, fresh water.

'I don't want my mother to know,' muttered Susie.

'What she thinks don't affect you, do it?'

Susie thought about it for a moment, wondering how he could think that. Of course her mother's thoughts affected her. And then Major reached out, took hold of the seat of Reuben's jeans in his long yellow teeth and bit. Reuben let out a howl of pain and rage. 'You _____ horse!'

Giggling, Susie turned and fled.

As the days passed Reuben Black became more and more settled. He started to run the yard his way. When it came to feeding he took no notice of Mrs Diamond's list, however much she explained it to him, and simply looked at the horses each day and decided this one looked well, that not so well, this one needed pepping up and that one slowing down. It seemed to work, and after several frustrating talks, when he just seemed to shrug and keep saying that he 'Give 'em what they look like', Mrs Diamond let him have his way. The horses were well and fit, even Diamond Bright. Especially Diamond Bright.

Reuben rode the horse every afternoon. He was Reuben's favourite, both Susie and her mother could tell. He would ride him out on hacks, jump him a bit, school him a bit, and spend hours in the stable grooming and strapping the gleaming chestnut coat. Diamond began to call to him when he came into the yard, and no longer whickered to Susie.

'We'll have to sell that horse soon,' said Mrs Diamond

one day, watching Reuben bring him back into the yard.

'Reuben won't like it,' said Susie.

Mrs Diamond sighed. 'I know. But we need the money. The boy's an extra mouth to feed and we must pay him something. And the roof needs mending and the car's playing up and the wagon's falling to bits. No, a horse has got to be sold. It has to be Diamond Bright.'

Even so, they might have waited. Mrs Diamond never got on with things right away. But that night a storm blew up and the rain came in heavy sheets, slapping down on the house. Susie found it hard to sleep, and kept getting up and looking out into the yard. Some of the doors were rattling against old, rusty catches, and she was worried the horses might get out. She was kneeling at the window when she felt drips on her hair. The roof was leaking again.

Soon there were buckets in her room, her mother's room and in the hall. The plink plink of dripping water was so loud that they put towels in the buckets to deaden the sound, turning it into a different, thlup thlup noise. Even so, it was hard to sleep, with the drips and the wind and the thought of streams of water trying to find a way down electric wiring and soaking ceilings to pulp.

In the morning Susie and her mother yawned miserably over their breakfast.

'It's no good,' said Mrs Diamond. 'We're going to have to sell that horse.'

Susie knew she would have to tell Reuben. She

thought about it all day at school, wondering when would be the right moment. She knew what it was like losing a horse you were fond of; Topic, her Shetland pony, had been sold when she grew too big, and her jumping pony, Dandelion, had disappeared once Mrs Diamond decided Susie needed something better. Horses came and horses went, and that was the way it had to be. But it was never easy.

Susie waited until it was getting dark, then went out into the yard. Reuben was doing his last check of the boxes, as he always did in the twilight. The storm seemed to have washed the weather clean and the night was warm, smelling of spring. There were even a few bats squeaking around the weathervane that stood on the old stable roof. Silently Susie followed Reuben round. At last they came to Diamond's box.

'Good lad, good lad,' crooned Reuben.

The horse snuffled the boy's jersey, blowing warm, scented air down his long nose.

'Aren't you the beauty?' laughed Reuben. 'Aren't you the one?'

'He is the one,' said Susie in a tight, hard voice. 'He's going to be sold.'

Reuben didn't speak. But he stopped stroking Diamond Bright's shining neck and closed his fingers into a fist. Then he turned abruptly away and went on around the boxes.

When he was done he stamped up to his loft. Susie followed, although he hadn't said that she could. The little room was neat and clean with nothing in it but a small pile of folded clothes. He had nothing, Susie realized, nothing at all.

'The good ones never stay,' he said suddenly.

'Don't they?'

'Nope. The bad ones stay for ever, can't give them away, but the good ones go.'

'Diamond Bright isn't good, not really. He's wild.'

'Not with me he ain't.'

'He is with me.'

'Stands to reason. You're scared.'

Susie took a deep breath. 'Yes,' she said. 'I am.'

Suddenly Reuben smiled at her. It changed his whole face. Most of the time he looked sullen, as if he expected someone to hit him or be unkind, but when he smiled he looked young, and mischievous, like a leprechaun or an elf. It was the first time he had smiled, thought Susie. He might grin, or even laugh, but he never smiled.

'I'll make us a drink,' he said, and went to put the kettle on.

They drank coffee, Reuben sitting on the bed and Susie on the one chair. They didn't talk, but it wasn't uncomfortable. Reuben wasn't much of a one for talking. At last, though, he said, 'Shouldn't sell Diamond. Do something, that horse will. Fetch a mint then.'

'Mum bred him to event,' said Susie. 'But we haven't anyone who can ride him.'

'I ride him. I can do it.'

'You?'

Susie almost gasped. Then she found herself struggling against laughter.

'Think I can't, do you? Think I can't ride?'

'No! No – it isn't that.' She put her hand up to try and pull her mouth out of its grin. Reuben was a natural on a horse, he could ride wonderfully, that wasn't the problem. No. It was just so hard to see him as an event rider, in the midst of all those well-off posh people. He was short and dirty, he smelled of horses all the time, he only had two pairs of jeans to his name. He couldn't read and he hardly spoke and when he did he was quite likely to swear, however many times Mrs Diamond told him off about it.

'I didn't really think of it as your sort of thing,' said Susie lamely.

'Don't like gypsy folk there, I daresay.' His face was closing again, shutting everything away. Like a flower when the sun goes in, thought Susie, although Reuben was nothing like a flower. He was a weed, really. Something nobody wanted.

Susie got up. 'I like gypsy folk,' she said firmly. 'And you're right, Diamond would make much more money if he was qualified as a novice eventer. I'll go and talk to my mother and tell her that she's got to start giving her eventing lessons to you and Diamond Bright.'

'You won't do that for me!' Reuben's face told her he didn't believe her.

'I will. I'll do it now.' She made for the ladder.

'You do that for me,' called Reuben after her, 'and I'll do something for you, too. Just you watch.'

Susie wondered if he could mend the roof. It was what they needed, after all.

Chapter Three

Susie kept on at her mother for days. 'We can start with hunter trials,' she said, waving schedules under her mother's nose. 'People are bound to see Diamond and be interested, but we won't sell him then. We'll wait until he's doing really well, and then we'll ask thousands.'

'The horse could be hurt. Then we'd have nothing to sell.'

'He's tough as old boots! Anyway, we ought to take the risk. Daddy would. He wouldn't say we shouldn't try.'

Mrs Diamond closed her eyes quickly. Susie knew she had upset her, talking of Daddy always did. But then her mother turned round and said, quite gently, 'It ought to be you riding Diamond, Susie. You used to ride so well. And what about Reuben? He couldn't event. He'll do the cross country all right, he's like a monkey on the horse, but can you imagine the dressage? It could take years to get him to any sort of standard. And we'll have to buy him clothes and make sure he doesn't upset anyone – I don't feel up to it, Susie. I'm too tired. Can't we just sell Diamond and have the roof mended and stop worrying every time it rains?'

Susie took a deep breath. 'I'll do all the organizing,' she said eagerly. 'I'll get him some things to wear, make the entries, everything. All you have to do is give him lessons.'

'I don't know that there's any point. You know what he's like, Susie. He thinks riding is just getting the horse to do what you want, he doesn't think it matters how you do it. To him a halt is a halt, but in a dressage test it's got to be a *good* halt. He doesn't understand.'

'I'll make him understand,' said Susie. 'He will. I promise he will.'

But it was easy to promise and much harder to make that promise work. Susie sat on the gate and bit her nails while her mother tried to teach Reuben and Diamond Bright dressage.

'Sit *up*, Reuben,' yelled her mother. 'Elbows *in*! Look straight *ahead*, not at the floor, *feel* that rein and come in from A. I said A. A! The cone with A on it! The other side, you foolish boy!'

Susie's heart sank. Reuben couldn't even read the letters of the dressage arena. The lesson went on and Mrs Diamond became more and more annoyed. Finally, she flung her hands in the air and gave up.

'I can't teach someone who won't learn!' she declared.

'I can learn,' said Reuben. But he looked miserable and cowed.

'Could you learn the test if someone showed you?'

demanded Mrs Diamond. 'Perhaps that's the way to start.'

'Aye,' said Reuben doubtfully, but Mrs Diamond turned to Susie at once.

'Right, Susie, up you get and show Reuben what to do.'

It was as if Susie had unexpectedly swallowed a huge piece of ice. Her heart went cold, her whole insides seemed to freeze. She felt as if all the blood in her body had stopped moving round. 'I can't ride Diamond,' she whispered, her lips stiff.

'Of course you can! He can't run off in the school, jump up on him at once! He's not a wicked horse, just spirited. And it's time you got over your fall.'

She had no choice. Reuben stood holding the horse, looking at her oddly. He said something but she didn't hear what it was. Her ears were filled with a dull roaring noise, like a train or a waterfall. All she could see was Diamond Bright, fresh, alert. Waiting. Little flecks of foam fell from his lips. The muscles of his shoulder were like hills covered with gleaming satin. Susie had never been able to hold him.

It's only the school, she told herself. I'll be all right in the school. But she looked at the strong wooden fence and wondered what it would be like to fall on that. The horse could step on her, crushing her bones. She could fall and be dragged, she might be killed. She could be crippled, and never walk properly again.

Her mother's lips moved, telling her to hurry. She took the crash hat and fastened it with stiff fingers, and then she was mounting, so easily, as she had done a thousand times before. Once in the saddle she felt almost calm. Now there was no escape.

At first Diamond was good. He walked and trotted in all the right places.

'Sit into him, Susie,' called Mrs Diamond. 'You've got to be part of the horse. Relax. Let him do the work.'

The horse blew down his nose and shook his head. Susie tensed in response, waiting for the buck, the shy, anything.

'At the next mark, canter,' called Mrs Diamond.

Susie's teeth met together, hard. She had to do what her mother wanted. She must. She sat down in the saddle, squeezed with her legs – and Diamond exploded.

He bucked like a bronco in a rodeo, legs stiff, head down, back in a steep curve. Susie hung on until the third buck and then flew off, to land with a thud in the soft dirt of the school. The horse bucked on, until finally, realizing he was free, he ran to the side of the school and hung his head, ashamed.

Mrs Diamond, who for a moment had been terrified for her daughter, launched into an angry tirade. 'What do you do to that horse, Susie? I've never seen anything so foolish in my life! Can't you even give the simplest of aids?'

Susie looked up and saw Reuben, small, dirty, watching her with his small, knowing eyes. He hadn't fallen off.

'I did try,' she muttered.

'You didn't try at all!' said her mother. 'You're going to ruin that horse. That's it, I've decided. We're going to sell him and be done.'

She stormed off into the house.

Reuben said plaintively, 'Would have been all right if I'd had some reading.'

'I hope that horse breaks a leg,' said Susie, rubbing her arm. She felt shaky, as she always did after a fall.

'Weren't the horse's fault,' said Reuben. 'He knows you're scared, even if your mother don't. Upsets him.'

'What's he got to be upset about? I'm the one that gets hurt.'

'Worries him, knowing you're scared. Thinks there's something he don't know. Lion maybe.'

'We'd have reason to worry if there was a lion about!' Susie almost laughed.

'Aye. That's what he thinks.'

Susie took a long, deep breath, letting the fear drain right out of her. She felt better, despite the bumps and bruises. Diamond Bright took a step or two towards them, wanting to be told everything was all right after all. He almost seemed to be saying sorry. Susie couldn't hate him, just because he was a horse she couldn't ride.

'We can't let her sell him, you know.'

'Looks like she's going to,' said Reuben.

'But I could teach you the letters in the ring,' said Susie excitedly. 'And the words you'd need at a hunter trial or an event. Start, Finish, Secretary, that sort of thing. In fact, I could teach you to read.'

'Horse'll be long gone,' said Reuben, and went to catch him and lead him away.

Susie trotted beside him as he walked back to the yard. 'I'll stop her somehow,' she said. 'We'll waste time. I'll offer to take the advertisement into the newspaper office and I'll forget. That gives us just over a week.'

'A week? To learn to read?'

Susie shrugged. 'It isn't hard,' she said.

But it was hard. Reuben was so sure he couldn't do it. He told Susie he had been to school for odd days here and there, never the same school and never for more than a week or two. There had been different teachers and different books, all confusing him. When Susie went up into the attic and got out the easy books from when she was little, he seemed to go stiff with horror.

'Can't,' he said, pushing them away.

'Yes, you can! Just look at the words, Reuben. The pictures tell you what they say.'

'Don't need words if you've got the pictures.'

'They're to help you. I'm helping you. Now, see this letter? What sound does it make?'

Suddenly he turned on her and his eyes blazed with fury. 'I don't need no ___ reading! I don't need no teaching! I get by!'

'You didn't today,' said Susie. 'And you won't at the hunter trial. I'm going to get in terrible trouble for stopping that advertisement, and I think the least you can do is try. Come on, Reuben! Just look at the words and try.'

He could read, a little, she discovered. But for some reason he thought there must be some secret he didn't know, something that meant people could look at words and know what they said without all the trouble he had in working them out.

'It's only practice,' said Susie. 'Look at this word, Start. You know that now, don't you? And people who can read just know lots more words. Anyone can do it.'

'Not me,' said Reuben.

'Yes, you,' said Susie. 'If you try.'

The next evening was better, but the third was worse. Reuben had bought a newspaper and kept trying to read words like 'enough' or 'group'.

'This is what they mean by trying to run before you can walk,' said Susie. 'You don't need those words yet.'

'I'm too stupid to need them, you mean! I'm a gypsy and we don't have no understanding. I know what you think.' Reuben was angry again, and kept getting up and walking about.

'I didn't say that. You just learn those words later. Reuben, will you please sit down!'

But sitting was almost the hardest part. He wasn't used to it, everything he did involved movement of some kind. Sitting made him restless and uncomfortable. On the fourth evening Susie pinned up the letters of the dressage arena all around his room, and made him walk from one to the other, and back, and across. She made him canter, and trot, and turn and rein back, and because he was moving, he understood.

Finally, he stopped. 'Right then,' he said. 'Know that, I do. No more reading.'

'You don't know anything yet,' said Susie.

'Know enough. That's it. Don't need no more.'

'Oh yes, you do. You haven't even begun.'

He made a face at her. 'Sound like your mum, you do. Can't boss me around.'

Susie got to her feet and picked up the books, slapping them together noisily. If he wanted to stay stupid that was all right with her. She didn't have to spend her evenings teaching him, trying to save Diamond.

'Don't matter, reading,' said Reuben, as she made for the door. 'Don't have to spend all our time studying,' he added, as she climbed down the ladder. And she heard him call, 'Susie!' as she stalked away across the yard.

Susie wasn't expecting her mother to find out about the advertisement until the weekend, so when she came home from school the next day and found her mother waiting for her with a face like thunder she wondered for a moment what she had done.

'Susie! Did you deliberately fail to take that advertisement in?' Susie opened and closed her mouth, making no sound at all, but Mrs Diamond didn't seem to need a reply. 'I telephoned today to check that it was displayed properly, only to discover that it was never received! Sometimes I think you are deliberately trying to make my life difficult! I work as hard as I can, do my absolute best and all you can do is frustrate me at every turn! Well, you can do without your supper. Go to your room at once!'

Susie went upstairs as slowly as she could.

Sometimes when her mother sent her to her room she changed her mind before she was all the way there. But not tonight. Mrs Diamond was furious.

As she sat on her bed, wishing she had had the sense to buy some chocolate from the school shop, just in case this happened, she heard a car arrive. Looking out of the window she saw that it was Mr Barnstaple, Major's owner. He was dressed in jodhpurs and had clearly come for a ride.

Oh, dear. Major hadn't been out today because Mr Barnstaple wasn't expected. The horse would be in one of his sour moods. Poor Mr Barnstaple.

She watched as her mother came out and tried to persuade Mr Barnstaple not to bother. She could see her smiling and pushing at her hair, talking too quickly. But he seemed determined, because soon they were fetching saddle and bridle and getting ready to go. The evening was dull and it looked as if it might rain, so Mr Barnstaple put on a brand new yellow riding mac. It flapped when he moved, making Major snort.

No sooner had Mr Barnstaple ridden from the yard than Mrs Diamond started shouting, 'Susie! Susie, get down here at once!'

Susie rushed down the stairs and into the kitchen. Her mother was looking frantic.

'Tom Barnstaple's gone off with Major and they're bound to have a disaster. He would wear that mac, and you know what Major's like about things that flap. Go after them on your bike, Susie, please. If the worst happens you can run for help.'

'I'll call the ambulance,' said Susie.

'Do you think we should? Just in case?'

Susie almost laughed. 'Not now! If he gets hurt.'

Mrs Diamond sat down, looking worried and upset. 'Oh. Yes. I suppose we'd better wait until then.'

Susie got her bike and rode down the lane at top speed, splashing through puddles and soft earth, turning on to the bridle path that led behind the church. Major's big hooves were easy to follow, the marks lumpy and uneven where Mr Barnstaple had urged the horse into a trot. Nothing seemed to have happened, and Susie wondered if it was worth going on.

Just then she heard the sound of thundering hooves. She stopped pedalling and stood in the middle of the path, holding her bike. Round the bend and into sight, heading at breakneck speed for home, came Major, without Mr Barnstaple. Reins flying, stirrups flailing, his face set in a scowl, the horse raced towards Susie.

It occurred to her to dive into the hedge. But at the end of the path was the road, and much as she hated Major she couldn't bear to think of him charging out in front of a lorry. What's more, he might hurt someone. She flung down her bike, spread out her arms and yelled, 'Whoa!'

The horse dived to the right, but Susie leaped at him. For a dreadful second she thought he was going to run her down, but at the last moment he slithered to a halt, turned and ran a few yards back the way he had come.

'Whoa! Whoa! Steady,' said Susie, her voice becoming gentle. She knew the horse was beside himself. In a few moments he would calm down and let her catch him.

Only when she had the reins firmly in her hand did she let herself think of Mr Barnstaple. Poor Mr Barnstaple, he might be hurt, dead, anything. Why hadn't she let her mother call the ambulance? She pulled the unwilling horse back down the track, urging him into a trot.

'Come on, you horrible creature! Show me what you did to him. And don't think you're getting any oats for supper, it's bran and carrots for you!'

Worried by the threat, Major blew down his nose and shambled along after her. If Susie hadn't been so worried she might have smiled. The horse was like a big, bullying boy, going on and on being nasty until someone slapped him and told him to behave. Major wasn't very clever, thought Susie. Perhaps she would have liked him better if she had realized that he simply didn't have much brain.

They met Mr Barnstaple limping along the track. His riding mac was covered in mud and his face was scratched. When he saw Susie he beamed with relief.

'Thank goodness you've got him! I thought he might get on to the road and be hurt.'

'I stopped him on the path,' said Susie. 'What did he do?'

Mr Barnstaple looked mystified. 'I don't really know. One minute we were trotting, the next he sort of jumped — and I was in a bush. Did something frighten him, do you think?'

'It could have done,' said Susie. 'It might have been your mac. Do you want to ride him back?'

'Er – no, I don't think I will. To tell the truth I'm a bit shaken. Shall we walk back together?'

Mr Barnstaple wheeled Susie's bike while Susie led the horse, and they chatted about school and horses and the stables. He was an easy, comfortable companion. She found herself telling him how she had stopped Major in his tracks, and about her father, and Reuben, and even Diamond Bright.

He said, 'You're an amazing girl, Susie. The things you take on. The horses, and your school work, and teaching this boy.'

Susie said, 'It's only because I have to. We don't have—' She stopped herself. She had been going to say 'much money', but she never told anyone they were poor. So instead she said, 'We don't have a lot of help.'

'You work too hard. Your mother too, she looks quite worn sometimes. Is Major too much bother, do you think?'

'No!' lied Susie at once. 'Not at all. We all love Major.'

It was getting dark by the time they reached home. Her mother and Reuben were in the yard, and Mrs Diamond rushed across to take Mr Barnstaple into the house and give him a cup of tea.

'I am so terribly sorry, Tom,' she said anxiously. 'We really must give Major more work. Susie can ride him for you. Can't you, Susie?'

'Hasn't Susie got enough to do?' asked Mr Barnstaple.

Susie opened her mouth to say yes, then caught her mother's eye. 'No,' she lied. 'I – I like riding Major.'

'Of course she does,' said Mrs Diamond, and hurried Mr Barnstaple into the house to fuss him and feed him cake.

Susie felt sick. Even if she didn't hate Major he was still hard to ride. When she put him to bed he put his ears down and looked at her mournfully, and she said, 'You needn't try that. I know I can't trust you.'

Reuben put his head over the door. 'I'll ride him,' he said.

Susie glanced round. 'It's all right. You haven't time.'

'Make time, won't I? Besides, we're turning horses out this week. Not so much work.'

'You don't have to,' said Susie. 'I'm not cross any more. And I liked helping you, I don't need paying back.'

He looked scornful. 'This ain't paying back! When you get paid back you'll know it.'

Susie was puzzled. But it was late and she had to go in. When she entered the kitchen her mother beamed at her unexpectedly.

'Susie! Look what Mr Barnstaple left for you. Ten pounds! For being so kind.'

'Ten pounds! Wonderful! Now we can enter Diamond and Reuben in the hunter trial!'

Mrs Diamond sighed. 'You don't give up, do you? Oh, all right then, if it means so much to you. On Saturday we'll take them to the hunter trial.'

Susie felt a great bubble of happiness and excitement growing inside her. Diamond Bright was the best horse they had ever had, and Saturday was only the beginning.

Chapter Four

When Susie woke on Saturday the day was bright, with a frost turning the weathercock on the stable roof white. She felt excited and happy. This was to be Diamond's day.

She ran downstairs and out into the yard. Reuben was sweeping up and he lifted his head briefly.

'Tell your mum I ain't going,' he said sourly.

Susie stopped in her tracks. 'Not going? But you must!'

'No must about it. Do what I want. Don't want to do that.'

Susie looked at him. If she hadn't known how brave he was she would have thought he was scared. But nothing about horses scared Reuben, nothing at all. He was shy though, she knew that. His gruff manner was only a front.

'I'll do any reading you can't,' she said. 'You don't have to worry. You don't have to talk to anyone if you don't want.'

'Think I'm a dummy, do you?'

Susie said nothing.

When he had finished sweeping, Reuben put the

broom away. Susie stood, waiting to see what he would do. He scowled at her.

'What you waiting for? Horse to be got ready. Think he can do it himself?'

'No – no.' Susie ran to fetch the travelling bandages for Diamond's precious legs.

The hunter trial was on a farm about ten miles away. Diamond Bright was a good traveller, and loaded happily enough into the shabby old wagon. Mrs Diamond drove, nursing the engine on all the hills.

'I don't know how we'll manage when the wagon's finished,' she said worriedly. 'We'll never be able to replace it.'

'We will when Diamond's famous,' said Susie happily. 'And he will be. Won't he, Reuben?'

Reuben, slumped in jeans and patched jumper, said nothing.

He walked the course while Susie did the entries. Mrs Diamond saw lots of people she knew and wandered around talking, catching up with news of old friends. But when Susie got back to the box she found Reuben sitting in the corner in a heap.

'Didn't you see the clothes I brought?' said Susie. 'You've got to change.'

Reuben looked up. 'You was right from the first,' he said. 'I shouldn't never have come. Likes of me don't belong.'

Susie looked out at the bustling crowds of people in their horsey clothes, with their expensive cars and well-fed dogs and noisy children. Reuben was right. He didn't belong.

'Even if you don't, Diamond does,' she said. 'He's the best horse here. Come on, Reuben, get changed. I'm the one that's supposed to be scared, remember?'

Right up to the last minute she thought he would back out. The jumper she had found for him was too short and too tight, and he hated the number tied around his waist. He looked uncomfortable and ill at ease, not at all like the Reuben they knew at home. Susie tried not to babble, tried to let him take his time, tried to let him gain confidence from Diamond Bright.

The horse looked wonderful in the sunshine. His coat gleamed with health and vitality, and he turned his lovely head this way and that, watching everything. Susie felt a great wave of pride; they had bred Diamond, had worried about him and loved him right from his very first moments of life. It didn't matter that she was too scared to ride. Even if he did nothing today, and she knew he would, she would never stop feeling proud.

It was time for Reuben to mount. Susie held Diamond's head while Reuben swung into the saddle. The moment she let go the horse danced sideways, half-rearing in his excitement. Susie's stomach fell away. How awful for Reuben. Suppose the horse reared up, suppose it fell back on him? Suppose the jumps were too much, or the horse bolted, or slipped and crushed him? She imagined everything, every horrible calamity. But Reuben, for the first time that day, was grinning.

'Down here, is it?' he said. 'You look sick as a dog, you do.'

'You just go to the end and through the gate,' said Susie. 'Warm him up in that paddock and wait until they call you. Number sixteen.'

Reuben gathered his reins and sent Diamond trotting bouncily down to the collecting ring.

As the riders went by, one after the other, Susie's heart began to pound. She could see her mother on the other side of the field talking to one of the organizers of the trials, waving her hands a lot, which showed that she too was nervous. Reuben kept Diamond on his own in the corner, kept him trotting and working, this way and that. The horse could be killed, thought Susie. Reuben could be killed. Oh, whose was this horrible idea?

At last it was Reuben's turn. Diamond Bright was snorting with excitement, his shoulder and neck already flecked with sweat. 'Take it steady, lad,' said the starter. 'He looks a handful. Now, three – two – one – go!'

They were off. Two plain fences and then a V of logs. You could either jump each leg of the V or take a leap across the point, and Diamond never hesitated. He flew the big fence and was away up the hill, jumping straw bales and tyres as if they weren't there.

A wall made him think, with a drop on the landing side, and he peered and snorted at a fence made of barrels painted red and white. Reuben drove him on, glued to the saddle, as much part of the horse as the mane or tail. Susie was speechless with excitement. She couldn't even cheer.

Diamond raced along, jumping the last few fences almost casually. A woman next to Susie said to her friend, 'That boy's a real jockey. The horse needs a bigger course, though. He's one to watch, mark my words. He's going to go far.'

Susie's heart ceased its pounding and began singing. Yes, she thought, yes. Diamond Bright is going to go far.

They won a rosette and a tiny silver cup. Mrs Diamond was so pleased she could hardly speak, only turning round to Reuben suddenly and saying, 'Thank you, thank you, Reuben. It's all down to you.' She rushed away to receive congratulations, everyone telling her how well she had done to breed such a horse and find such a boy to ride him.

''Tweren't just me,' said Reuben to Susie. 'Was you as well. Showing me how to go on, like.'

Susie shrugged. 'I suppose she takes me for granted. After all, I'm always around.'

Reuben grunted. Not for the first time, Susie wished she knew what he was thinking. She knew him well enough to know he was thinking something.

Together, they bandaged Diamond for the journey home, washing out his mouth with warm water and bathing his eyes. He was so tough and fit that the outing had hardly tired him at all, he looked as if he could do the same again, backwards.

Susie grinned at the horse. 'I like you much better

now I don't have to ride you,' she told him. 'I didn't mean all the things I said to you.'

He looked down his long nose and blew into her hair. He had known Susie all his life, she was part of his small world.

Susie put her arms round his neck. 'It could have been me, today,' she whispered. 'Why were you so naughty, Diamond Bright?'

The horse pulled away, as he always did. It was just his nature, thought Susie. A tough, clever horse needed a tough, clever rider, someone he could respect. Diamond might love her but her nerves and timidity had spoiled things; she would never ride Diamond as Reuben had done today.

All that evening and for days afterwards people kept telephoning Mrs Diamond asking to buy Diamond Bright. To begin with Susie thought she might agree, but she always said no.

'You were right,' she told Susie. 'He's going to event. He's a wonderful horse.'

Each day after that Mrs Diamond worked with Reuben, trying to teach him dressage. Sometimes, after school, Susie sat on the fence and watched them. Now, thanks to her, Reuben knew all about extending and collecting at the trot, he understood the half halt, could work on two tracks, and didn't look cross every time Mrs Diamond called out, 'Halt at A, please, and rein back five paces.'

If only he would sit up more in the saddle. He was like a jockey in some ways, crouched over the horse's withers, leathers short, balance perfect. When Diamond played up, as he always did when he got bored, Reuben never once looked in any danger. But somehow, together, the pair lacked elegance. Susie had seen hundreds of dressage tests and she knew this workmanlike, good enough performance wasn't going to win any prizes. No, Reuben and Diamond were never going to be really good at dressage. To make up, they would just have to be brilliant across country.

This was where Reuben excelled. In the old days, before her accident, Mrs Diamond had built cross-country fences into all the field boundaries. Over the years they had become broken-down and useless, but now, fired with new enthusiasm, she and Reuben together pulled old logs across the gaps and redug ditches, until they could practise everything they might meet at a novice event. Ditches, walls, drops, bounce jumps with just one stride in between, everything was there.

'Remember, Reuben,' Mrs Diamond said, 'lots of cross-country horses go round three parts out of control. Sooner or later those horses are going to fall. Your horse has to attack the fences with courage, but you must have control. He must do absolutely what you ask, however excited he is.'

Reuben grunted, as he always did. It was hard to curb Diamond's enthusiasm, the more he jumped the more he relished jumping and the wilder he became. The only answer was patience and work, jumping until the horse was bored by it, working in circles and figures of eight until Diamond instinctively obeyed Reuben's aids. He worked so hard, thought Susie. He even found time in the day to ride Major, just so that she wouldn't have to. Even if he denied it, perhaps that was what he meant by paying her back. She had helped him to succeed with Diamond, and he was helping her.

Then, one evening, when her homework was done and she came out into the yard to see the horses and feed the cats, Reuben stamped towards her and said, 'Got the books, then?'

Susie blinked. 'I thought you'd given up all that.'

'Taking a rest, weren't I?' He put his hands in his pockets and shot her small, wary glances.

'You said you knew enough,' said Susie. 'I suppose you've decided you don't.'

Reuben said nothing for a moment. Then he admitted, 'There's things I don't know.'

'You'd better not swear at me again,' said Susie.

'Didn't.'

'Did!'

He made a face. 'You and your ma! Hoity-toity Miss La-di-Da!' He walked on tiptoes, pretending to be a posh lady in high heels. Susie laughed and went to get the books.

After that they read most nights. The books were funny though, about elves and fairies and little children saying, 'Here we are, this is my dog Spot.' Sometimes Susie almost burst out laughing, thinking what her friends would say if they saw her. But then she looked at Reuben crouched over the page, his dirty finger moving along the words, struggling to make out the letters, and she didn't think it was funny at all. No wonder he couldn't learn at school, she thought. Everyone must have laughed at him so much.

'You won't tell no one, will you?' he said to her one night, just as she was packing up.

'Reuben! You know I won't!'

'Girls are like that. Always talking.'

'I'm not like that,' said Susie. 'I don't tell tales. I wouldn't even tell Ellen.'

And she didn't tell Ellen. It was just that somehow Ellen found out. Susie hadn't meant it to happen, but one day she was opening her locker when a book fell out. She had borrowed it from the school library, from a series for very slow readers called 'Reading Made Easy'. It was about this boy in the Middle Ages who ran away to sea on a sailing ship, and Susie thought Reuben might find it more interesting than Spot the Dog.

'What's this?' asked Ellen. 'Oooh, isn't it hard? "Look, look, here is a ship! It is a big ship. It has big red sails." What on earth do you want this for, Susie?'

'Give it here.' Susie snatched it back and stuffed it in her bag.

Ellen said, 'Is it a secret? You can tell me, can't you? I'm your best friend.'

'No,' said Susie more abruptly than she intended. 'I can't tell anyone, so don't ask.'

Ellen's neck went very red, which meant she was upset. Susie reached out and touched her arm, meaning to apologize, but Ellen shook her off. Susie felt like crying. She had snapped at Ellen too often lately, just as her mother snapped at her, for no better reason than that Ellen was there. Ellen was the dearest friend she had ever had, and now she might go off with Naomi Fisher or anyone.

She hated Naomi Fisher. The girl never missed a chance to be mean. Susie tried to ignore her, but it was hard when they travelled on the same bus, and even harder when Naomi rode over for a lesson with Susie's mother. Naomi's father bought her glossy, expensive ponies with frail legs and hot temperaments, and after a few weeks they had to be weighed down with double bridles and standing martingales so that Naomi could ride them at all. Mrs Diamond said it wasn't surprising. Naomi had a poor seat and was far too free with her stick.

But Naomi had a house full of videos and gadgets, and Naomi's mother never gave anyone sandwiches for tea; she took them out to cafés and bought burgers, because, as she said, 'Naomi's little friends are always welcome. Would you like another milkshake, dear? Ice-cream? Chocolate?' Everyone wanted to be Naomi's friend.

Susie said, 'I'd tell you if I could,' in a pleading voice. 'I can't. Honestly. It's not my secret.'

'You're teaching someone to read,' said Ellen slowly. 'And – I know who it is! It's Reuben, isn't it? He's a gypsy and hasn't learned to read.'

Susie went red.

Ellen said, 'There! I am right. And I think it's mean of you not to tell.'

'He said I shouldn't,' said Susie. 'He's embarrassed.'

'I should think so! Sixteen and never learned to read. I suppose it's because gypsies never go to school. Don't worry,' she added, seeing Susie's anxious face. 'I won't tell.'

Susie was almost sure she wouldn't, though she knew Ellen wasn't always good at keeping secrets. She felt anxious suddenly. Only a few months ago she and Ellen had seemed so close. They used to be able to tell each other anything, and now they had to watch what they said. Susie wondered if it was her fault. All the problems at home had seemed too painful to discuss, even with Ellen, and there wasn't the time there used to be, to listen to music together, or go into town. She supposed that she had shut Ellen out. She would make it better, she decided, when she had time. Thinking of what she could do to make up with Ellen, Reuben and the reading were forgotten.

Chapter Five

One day Susie got off the school bus and walked up the long drive to the house, only to see a small, dark man standing talking to Reuben. When they saw her they parted, and the dark man slipped away through the field gate, disappearing over the hill almost before Susie realized. One second he was there and the next he was gone. She blinked. It was almost as if she had imagined him.

'Was that someone you know?' she asked Reuben.

'Who?'

'That man. The man you were talking to.'

'Didn't see no one.' He turned his back, picked up a broom and started sweeping. She knew he wasn't going to tell her.

She saw the man again one morning, a morning so bright that the sun shone through the curtains and woke her early. She lay in bed for a moment or two, thinking how different life was since Reuben came. No more rushing, no more feeling as if the world was about to come crashing down on her head. There still wasn't any money but nowadays Susie wasn't always in trouble. It used to be trouble at home because the work needed doing, and trouble at school because of bad marks and work she hadn't done, and nothing anywhere in between. But her marks were good this term. And without the horrible, horrible riding she could love the horses once again.

She leaned from her window to take a breath of fresh morning air. And there was the man. He was crossing the yard with that quick, sliding stride he had, as if he was slipping away before he was noticed. In a moment he was gone.

Susie felt her happy mood evaporate. Reuben didn't steal, she knew that. But this man might be an old friend, and friends couldn't always be trusted. What was he doing here in the early mornings, why didn't he want to be seen? She got dressed quickly and hurried down to the yard. A quick glance round the tack room told her that all the saddles were in place. An empty rack would be noticed at once. What about the bridles, though? There were so many, and some of the livery owners took theirs home to clean. The man could have taken rugs, bridles, anything.

Suddenly, she thought of something. The man had been carrying nothing more than a cloth bag, the sort of bag men used to carry pheasants they had shot. She put a hand to her mouth. That must be it. Pheasants. Reuben's friend must be a poacher!

She waited until Reuben came back from exercising Diamond. The horse was sweated up and Reuben gave him a brisk rub down before putting a sweat rug on. Steam rose in clouds, and Diamond stamped his feet restlessly, as tired horses will.

'I saw your friend,' said Susie. 'And don't worry, I won't tell. About the pheasants.'

Reuben looked at her sideways. 'You didn't see no pheasants.'

'I saw the bag. And I can guess what's in it. I bet he got them from Far Wood.'

'Guessing ain't proof.' Suddenly he turned and said fiercely, 'You mind your own business, Miss Curious. That aren't your business. And if Danny gets some pheasants for doing a kindness, that aren't anyone's business but the pheasants', lessen the keeper finds out.'

Susie was puzzled. 'Didn't that man take the pheasants, then?'

'I aren't saying,' said Reuben, and folded his lips in a way that told Susie he wouldn't say another word.

But when Diamond was settled he turned and said, 'Come see what Danny brought, then.'

Puzzled, Susie followed him. He went through the field gate and over the hill, then down to the stream and up again to the little paddock out of sight of the house. They didn't use it much, because it was scrubby and didn't have good grass, but it was sheltered. Sometimes old horses were put there in the summer, if they were resting. The fence was just rickety timber, there were cowslips in the long tufts of meadow grass, and small spotted toads lived in the damp patches under the hedge.

A horse was in the field. If you could call it a

horse. Not very big, perhaps 14.3, feet like dinner plates and head like a hammer. What's more it was a horrible dirty grey, with black spots here and there, as if someone had left it under a tree dripping black slime. Its mane stood up like a very old brush, and it blinked long, lazy lashes over its deep blue eyes.

'Yuk!' said Susie.

'Told you I'd pay you back,' said Reuben, happily.

'With this?' Susie stared from him to the horse and back again. 'I don't need paying back! And what do I want with something so ugly? My mother's going to send it to the knacker the moment she lays eyes on the thing.'

'She ain't going to lay eyes on her,' said Reuben calmly. 'Not yet. Not till you see what she's like. Come here, Doris. Come here. Come and talk to us.'

Doris lifted her big head and ambled over. She had a pink nose and pink eyelids. She was the ugliest horse Susie had ever seen in all her life.

'Say hello to Susie, Doris,' said Reuben.

Doris blew down her nose, and snuffled.

'You're horrible,' said Susie, finding a mint in her pocket and giving it to the mare.

'Don't do to judge by appearances,' said Reuben.

'I don't want a horse,' said Susie. 'I've given up on horses.'

'Don't do to say things you don't mean,' said Reuben.

Susie felt cross with him suddenly. He was always watching her with those black button eyes, watching and thinking. She didn't want people to think about her, especially someone like Reuben.

'I can get a hundred horses better than this,' she snapped. 'I've never seen such a mess!'

'There's no horse better than Doris,' said Reuben. 'Try her.'

'I don't want to ride.'

'You don't want to ride bad horses. Never tried Doris.'

'I haven't time!'

'Getting to be summer. Lots of time in summer. Scared of her, are you?'

She was, but she wouldn't admit it. No one could be scared of a horse like this. She scowled at the boy. 'Oh – very well! One ride. That's all. Just one.'

She stormed back to the house for her hat. A familiar, nasty sensation was welling up in the pit of her stomach. It was almost, but not quite, like feeling sick, and a little like excitement, although it definitely wasn't that. What's more her hands were wet suddenly, and she was breathing in short, quick bursts, and that in turn made her ears ring and her heart pound as if something terrible was going to happen. It's only a horse, she told herself. A stupid, ugly, dobbin of a horse. Nothing could happen to you on a horse like that. It wasn't Major, nor Diamond Bright, it was a quiet horse. An easy horse. She'd show Reuben she could ride!

But she felt worse and worse as she neared the top field. She imagined a horse the size of an elephant, and when she saw Doris she felt strange because she was so small. Such an ugly horse. Such a mess. But at least she wasn't very big.

Reuben had tacked Doris up with an old saddle and a plain snaffle bridle.

'I always like a martingale,' said Susie, her face stiff and uncomfortable. 'The neckstrap—'

'Doris don't need a martingale. And she don't mind if you hold her mane neither,' said Reuben. 'Doris don't mind what you do, so long as you don't fall off. Hates people falling off. Makes her all upset.'

Susie wondered if Doris trampled you when she was upset. If a foot got caught in the stirrup she might drag you for miles, until you were smashed to pieces against a rock. That was the sort of thing horses did. Even horses like Doris.

She adjusted the stirrups with quick fingers. It was odd, to be so good at something that frightened you so. She couldn't even remember when the fear had started, because at first it had been small and easily ignored. But the horses had got harder and the fear had grown, and now her hands were shaking and she wanted to cry, when it was only a stupid, ugly horse called Doris.

'Want a leg up?' said Reuben.

Susie shook her head. Her legs would hold her up, they must.

Gritting her teeth, she swung into the saddle.

Doris stood like a rock. Her ears pricked, interestedly. Susie gathered her reins and squeezed with her legs, and Doris moved smoothly into a long, relaxed walk. Susie was surprised. You didn't expect a horse like this to move well. After a minute or two, when she had tried turning Doris right and left, stopping, starting, and reining back, she decided to speed up. A gathering of the reins, a little squeeze, and Doris was bouncing along in her upright, jerky trot. Susie sat it, feeling her teeth rattle in her head, and decided to try rising. Much better.

'Put her into a canter,' called Reuben. 'That's her best pace.'

'No,' said Susie.

'Go on!' said Reuben.

'She might bolt.'

'What? Doris? Give over!'

Susie's teeth were clenched so tight that her jaw hurt. She had to do it. If she didn't, Reuben would know she was even scared of Doris. She sat down in the saddle, slipped her right leg behind the girth, turned the mare's head a little to the left and asked for a canter. The mare struck off like clockwork on her near fore. It was like being on a rocking horse, thought Susie. It was easy. It was fun. Sitting on that broad, solid back, rocking backwards and forwards, was as far from the terror of Diamond Bright as it was possible to be. Some of the tension eased out of her. She almost laughed.

'Nice old girl, Doris,' said Reuben as she pulled up.

'She goes well enough,' said Susie in surprise. 'Wonderfully schooled.'

'Danny knows how to school a horse,' said Reuben, almost smirking. 'Go jump that fence with her. Jumped bigger than that, Doris has.'

Susie eyed the fence, three feet high at least. 'You are making that up,' she said.

'Try her.'

'No! What do you think I am, stupid?'

'Must be. If you think old Doris can hurt you.'

'I'm not scared!'

'Go on, then. Jump the fence.'

Suppose she fell off, thought Susie. Suppose Doris reached down with her horrible yellow teeth and savaged her? Diamond had kicked her once, by accident, when she fell off, and Major bit like a shark if he got the chance. And jumping was the absolute worst. People got killed, jumping.

'Another day,' she said. 'When I'm a bit more used to her.'

To her relief, Reuben nodded.

Susie chose her moment to break it to her mother that they had acquired another horse. She waited until Mr Barnstaple had been, stopping in the kitchen after his ride, to have a cup of tea and hand over a cheque. Visits from Mr Barnstaple always put her mother in a good mood.

'I've been thinking,' Susie began. 'The far paddock's wasted, really. We ought to put something in it.'

'We'll get someone to put cows in, later on,' said her mother absently. 'We can't mow it. The wild flowers would suffer.'

'We could put a horse in it.'

'Too far to go.' Mrs Diamond sipped her tea. 'It hurts my leg, walking that far every day. This farm's really too big, you know, Susie. Perhaps we should sell that paddock. Let someone keep a horse in it.'

Susie took a deep breath. 'There's a horse in the

far paddock already,' she said in a rush. 'My horse. At least, Reuben's lent her to me. She's called Doris.'

Mrs Diamond blinked at her. 'You? A horse? What horse? Susie, why?'

Susie shrugged, helplessly. 'Reuben got her. I don't know why. I didn't ask him or anything.'

Her mother put down her tea cup and got to her feet. 'This I must see,' she said.

Because she knew her mother would hate Doris on sight, Susie picked up her riding hat, put the old saddle over her arm and slung a bridle across her shoulder. The load slowed her pace to her mother's, an awkward hobble over the tussocks of grass. When at last they reached the far paddock they rested, breathless, by the gate. Doris lifted her ugly head and whinnied.

'Oh no!' wailed Mrs Diamond. 'A gypsy horse!'

'She's very good natured,' said Susie. 'I mean, really. She isn't – I mean – oh, dear. Doris! Doris, come here.'

Doris ambled over, her great, feathery feet plodding into the earth. She went straight up to Susie and blew at her.

'Hello, Doris,' said Susie, thinking again what a horrible-looking horse she was.

'I have never seen such an equine disaster in all my life,' said Mrs Diamond incredulously. 'What can Reuben be thinking of? You can't ride this, Susie. She's all on the forehand and slow as anything. I admit, perhaps I've overhorsed you in the past, but this is ridiculous!'

'She's nice to ride,' said Susie in a small voice.

'Don't pretend, Susie! I know you like Reuben but we can't bend over backwards to make him happy. And think of where she comes from. She could be diseased, anything. She could threaten the health of the whole stable.'

'She looks well enough to me,' said Susie.

'She looks terrible! No, Susie, she's got to go.'

Susie looked at her mother's angry face. She wasn't really worried about disease, Susie could tell. It was just that she didn't want people to see her daughter on a horse like that. She thought it would look bad. People would think it was the best they could do.

A great stone seemed to have settled in Susie's stomach. She climbed doggedly over the fence, took up the saddle and plonked it on Doris's wide, white back. The pony stood stockstill, and when Susie showed her the bridle she opened her mouth helpfully.

'This isn't a horse, it's a teddy bear,' said Mrs Diamond scornfully. 'You can't keep her, Susie!'

But Susie put on her hat and fastened the chin strap. Then she swung up into the saddle and sent Doris into a trot, circling the lumpy field.

'Don't think you can bring her into the yard,' called Mrs Diamond. 'I won't have her near good horses!'

Susie didn't listen. The stone in her stomach was rattling up and down as she trotted, and as it rattled it dissolved a little. In a minute it was gone. There was just Doris, and the pain of muscles that were out of practice, trotting over the tussocky grass. She felt Doris leaning on the bit, and sat down a little more, using her legs to encourage the mare to put her back end to work and lift her head. Doris tightened up, doing her best to oblige. 'You good girl,' said Susie. 'You really are a very good girl.'

Mrs Diamond called out, 'That poor horse can't collect herself to save her life. She's useless, Susie!'

Susie set her teeth. She squeezed Doris into her lovely, rocking canter. She did figures of eight, at first putting two or three trot strides at the crossover. But she knew that only a flying change would impress her mother, and she was sure Doris could do it. She had to do it. She concentrated hard on getting the horse balanced, on timing her aid for the exact moment when Doris could bring her other leg through. This time. It had to be this time. Now! To her amazed delight, Doris changed, and went rocking away on the other leading leg.

'Good heavens! Well done, Susie. You can even teach that horse a thing or two.'

'She's a good horse,' called out Susie.

'She'll never be a good horse.'

Poor Doris! Susie looked at the big, plain ears on top of the big, ugly head and felt a surge of affection for poor, unloved Doris. 'We'll show her,' she muttered, and set Doris straight at the rickety fence.

'Susie! Don't! That horse can't jump!'

'Of course she can,' yelled Susie. But suddenly the fear came flooding back. Suppose Doris couldn't jump? Suppose Doris fell, and Susie with her, and never walked again?

'Susie! Susie, pull up at once!'

The fence was so close. Susie couldn't move a muscle, she was frozen with terror. She couldn't kick, she couldn't pull, she simply sat and waited for the worst.

'Susie!'

Doris saw the fence, waited for instructions, and when none came took charge. She gathered herself, sat back on her hocks and jumped. The rickety fence passed easily beneath them.

They stopped on the other side. Mrs Diamond hurried across the field towards them, her leg dragging and her face flushed.

'Susie! That was madness, you could have been hurt!'

'Yes. I know.' Susie climbed off the horse and stood, leaning against Doris's solid, too straight shoulder.

'I wouldn't have believed the horse could do it. That's three foot if it's an inch.'

'Reuben said she could jump.'

Mrs Diamond looked angry. 'I must have a word with that boy! He behaves as if he belongs around here and he's taking liberties. I won't have it.' Absently, Mrs Diamond reached out and patted Doris's hairy neck.

Susie put Doris back in her field and untacked her. Could the horse stay or not? Her mother still hadn't said. But as they were leaving, Mrs Diamond gave the mare an exasperated stare.

'Her face is going to be a bother,' she said crisply. 'I hope you're prepared to walk over here at least twice a day in summer, and put cream on her eyes and lips. A horse like that can get terrible sunburn.'

'She could come in a field nearer the house,' suggested Susie, but her mother glared.

'No she cannot. I don't want her where people can see. And if you meet anyone out riding, Susie, I want you to say she's a livery we're keeping for a very short while. I do not want people thinking that this is the sort of horse we keep. We're a high-class stable and nothing less.'

She began the long trudge back to the house. Susie stayed with Doris a moment, and mimicked her mother's voice.

'We're a high-class stable and nothing less!' They weren't so high class. They couldn't afford a good horse-box or decent tack, they were always in debt to the blacksmith and the feed merchant and if it wasn't for people like Mr Barnstaple, who didn't know a good horse from a bad one, they wouldn't be able to live. But she knew what her mother meant. People didn't send good liveries to stables with horses like Doris.

She stroked the mare's pink nose. Doris snuffled, and she wished she had brought her a titbit, so she reached under the fence and found some nice grass that Doris couldn't reach and gave her that. What a strange afternoon it had been. She thought of the jump, but it felt almost as if she'd imagined it. Only one thing was certain: for a few brief moments she had actually enjoyed riding Doris.

Chapter Six

Ellen was coming for tea, the first time in ages. She and Susie got off the school bus together, and Oliver called out, 'Going to watch our centaur perform, are you?'

Naomi Fisher sneered. 'Have fun, Ellen,' she said in mock sweetness. 'Don't have too much excitement.'

Susie went red, and walked quickly away down the track, with Ellen almost running to keep up. Ellen had gone to tea with Naomi Fisher only last week.

Reuben was in the yard. Ellen said, 'Hello,' and smiled, but Reuben took no notice. He didn't like strangers and he wouldn't talk to them. Even the liveries couldn't get a word out of him most days.

'He isn't very friendly,' muttered Ellen. 'And his clothes are a disaster! All in holes.'

'You shouldn't judge by appearances,' said Susie.

Ellen hunched a shoulder. She hadn't meant to criticize, only to say. Why wouldn't Susie talk about the gypsy? It was almost as if Susie was better friends with Reuben than with her.

But Susie was thinking differently. Suppose Ellen told Naomi Fisher that Reuben dressed in rags? Now that the weather was warmer and Reuben no longer wore his donkey jacket he looked a complete wreck. Both pairs of jeans had holes in them, to the point where they barely held together, and his T-shirts had washed to a uniform grey. But he wasn't so thin as he used to be. Mrs Diamond's cooking was filling him out nicely, which would have been fine except that now his clothes didn't fit.

'Are you still teaching him to read?' asked Ellen.

Susie turned on her. 'You're not to talk about that! Especially not to him. He'd think I'd told you everything.'

'You're supposed to tell best friends everything!' said Ellen crossly.

'Not if people don't want you to.'

Ellen didn't say anything. The two girls went up to Susie's bedroom. Ellen got some make-up out of her school bag, and put it on while Susie watched enviously. Ellen looked brilliant with make-up on, while Susie looked like a little girl dressing up, with none of the right colours.

'What do you think?' said Ellen, turning round.

'Great. Really.'

'Why don't you put some on?'

But Susie knew Ellen would laugh if she saw her own collection of cheap eyeshadows and ends of her mother's lipsticks. She didn't have the money to buy more. Ellen had special creams and lotions for young skin, paid for out of pocket money, but the only money Susie ever had was tips from liveries like Mr Barnstaple, and she saved those for entry fees.

Diamond's future was more important than make-up. So instead she said, 'Let's go and see Doris.'

It had rained earlier in the day and the grass was wet. Ellen complained that her shoes were soaking, and for a brief moment Susie wished that Ellen wasn't her friend. She wasn't the same as she used to be. They didn't seem to like the same things any more, and besides, there was Naomi Fisher. You couldn't trust someone you knew might talk to Naomi.

It was money, thought Susie miserably. Everyone else could buy make-up and tapes and clothes, and they had videos at home and went on holiday. All she had was Doris.

The mare came up and talked to them. Her long, silky lashes made Susie smile. Somehow everything about Doris made her smile.

'She's not very pretty,' said Ellen.

'She's pretty inside,' said Susie. 'Doris has a beautiful nature.'

'Can't say that it shows,' said Ellen, still in her scratchy mood.

Susie had an idea. 'Would you like a ride? She's very quiet.'

Ellen looked dubious. Then she shrugged. 'I don't suppose there's anything else to do.'

Nowadays, to save carrying things, Susie kept the bridle in a plastic bag under the hedge. As usual Doris opened her mouth for the bit and blinked her long eyelashes when Susie patted her. Ellen scrambled aboard from the fence. She had ridden up until last year, when she lost interest and gave up.

At first all went well, and Ellen called out and laughed. It's going to be all right, thought Susie. This is going to put Ellen in a good mood again. But suddenly and without warning, Ellen kicked the mare.

'Gee up, you old nag!' she shouted, and drummed her heels into Doris's sides, just as if she was an old riding-school pony with no feelings left. 'Gee up!'

The mare snorted a little.

'You don't have to kick her to death!' called Susie.

Ellen shouted, 'She needs waking up,' and kicked her again, hard.

Susie shuddered, almost feeling the thud of Ellen's heels in her own sides.

But Doris woke up all right. She leaped into a canter, almost leaving Ellen in a heap on the floor. No sooner had the girl recovered than with no warning at all, the mare turned on a sixpence, flicked her heels in the air and stopped.

This time Ellen slid over the horse's shoulder, and if Doris had chosen this spot she could not have chosen better. Ellen's bottom landed fair and square in a pile of fresh dung.

Doris lifted her head and stared at Susie with her large blue eyes. 'I will not have people taking liberties,' she seemed to say, and she walked slowly away up the field.

Susie was doubled up with laughter. She laughed so much she had to sit down.

Ellen, furious, jumped to her feet. 'This is all your fault!' she screamed. 'Now I stink almost as much as that boy! It's not funny. We're supposed to be friends!'

'I didn't mean you to fall off,' said Susie. 'You shouldn't have kicked Doris like that. She's sensitive.'

'Sensitive? She's so ugly she ought to be shot! And so are you. Stupid, ugly, Susie Diamond. And I'll tell you this for nothing, I won't ever be friends with you again!'

Susie stopped laughing. At first she thought Ellen didn't mean it, but then she saw that she did. She wanted to cry. Instead she folded her lips over her teeth and said nothing. Ellen stormed back to the house, washed, and telephoned her mother to come and get her. When she arrived Ellen got in the car and drove off without once looking back.

The break-up led to some horrible days for Susie. People stopped talking when she went into the classroom in the morning, and Ellen and Naomi Fisher would look at her, grin, and whisper something. Oliver, seeing that they sat apart on the bus, said, 'Oh, winds of war, is it? Come and sit next to me, Susie, and impress me with your horse-sense.'

Susie wouldn't. Both Ellen and Naomi Fisher fancied Oliver and would only hate her more. She sat by herself and stared out of the window and hoped everyone thought it was what she wanted to do.

At least not having a friend meant she had more time to teach Reuben. He was reading quite well now, and sometimes she took the evening paper up and he would try and read the racing page. Funnily enough, he found numbers quite easy. He understood betting odds better than Susie, who had never really worked out what it was all about.

'But you don't bet,' she said to him.

He shrugged. 'Me dad used to. I could take it up. Get bus into town, like, and see the bookie.'

'I don't think you're old enough,' said Susie. 'But if you've got some money you could go into town and buy clothes.'

He looked at her in that way he had, not quite straight.

'I'll come with you if you want,' she said. 'I like shopping.'

He didn't say anything. But on Saturday, when the liveries were on a long ride and the yard was swept, he washed his hands and smoothed his hair and said, 'Come on, then. Bus to catch.'

It was strange, being in town together. Susie noticed that when Reuben went into a shop all the assistants got anxious, as if he was going to cause trouble. But then, when they saw he was with her, they didn't mind any more. It was because he looked like a gypsy, she thought. She'd been the same, with Danny. If you looked like a gypsy everything you did was different.

In all the weeks Reuben had worked for them he had hardly spent a penny of his wages. They bought new jeans, T-shirts, a jacket and a couple of white shirts.

'If you're going to compete in events you'll need the shirts,' said Susie. 'We've got jodhpurs you can borrow, and my father's coats with the sleeves turned up, but you've got to have shirts.'

'When's it going to be, then? This event?'

Susie shrugged. 'When my mother thinks you're good enough, I suppose.'

When the shopping was done they went into McDonalds and bought a milkshake each and a portion of chips between them. But Susie felt dismal. Everyone seemed to have better clothes than she did; she just had ordinary jeans and ordinary jumpers, and when she was at the stables she didn't care. But town was different. She felt dowdy and plain.

Reuben was making a noise with his straw. Susie looked away, wishing he wouldn't, and out of the corner of her eye, she saw Ellen come in. She was with Naomi Fisher.

'Quick,' she said in a low voice to Reuben. 'Let's go.'

His eyes moved round the room quickly, passing over Ellen almost without looking at her. The gypsy way of looking. But he said, 'Aye. It's her. Let's go.'

They got up, but Susie was clumsy and knocked over her cup. Strawberry milkshake dripped on to the floor and someone yelled, 'Cloth here, please! Cloth!'

Naomi Fisher looked towards them. When she saw Susie her expression changed from boredom to devilish glee. 'Oh, look, Ellen,' she said loudly, 'it's Susie Diamond. The poor girl with the lame mother and all those unmanageable horses.'

Susie's cheeks flamed. She looked accusingly at Ellen, but Ellen avoided her gaze. At least she looked uncomfortable, thought Susie.

'And who's that with her?' carolled Naomi. 'Don't tell me it's the gypsy. He can't read, you know. Susie gets him baby books and tries to teach him to write his name!'

Reuben didn't say a word. But his face changed, somehow. It closed up on itself. Everyone was looking at him and he was just a gypsy, a dirty gypsy that couldn't read.

They rushed out of the restaurant into the street. When they got round the corner Susie caught his arm. 'I didn't tell. She just found the books in my bag.'

'You told,' said Reuben.

'I didn't! I swear I didn't!'

He stared at her then, and his face was cold and angry. 'My people always say we can't live in your world. Say there's no point in trying. Thought there was a point. Thought I could do the things you do. But there aren't no use in any of it. Keep your job. Keep your ____ event riding. I don't belong.'

He turned away and walked down the street. Susie would have gone after him, but suddenly she remembered all their parcels left in McDonalds. She would have to go back, past Ellen and Naomi Fisher.

When she walked in Ellen saw her and went bright red. She nudged Naomi, who turned, laughed, and called out, 'Hello, Susie dear! How's your boyfriend?'

Susie went and gathered up all her parcels, holding them in one hand so she could open the door. Ellen and Naomi whispered to each other and then burst out laughing. Reuben was so easy to laugh at, thought Susie. It was easy to gang up on people and make fun. She went slowly and deliberately towards Naomi's table. Each girl had a Big Mac, cheese oozing slightly at the edges.

'What do you want, Susie?' asked Naomi, rather nervously, Susie thought.

'This,' she said. She picked up the Big Mac, removed the top bun and squashed the rest carefully in Naomi's hair.

Chapter Seven

Reuben wasn't on the bus and he wasn't in the lane. The moment Susie reached home she ran up to his loft. He wasn't there either. What's more, his things were gone, the stained jeans, the old T-shirts, everything. The reading books and the newspapers were piled up on the table, neatly. But Reuben was gone.

She did the afternoon feed without him and then the evening feed as well.

'Where's Reuben? Is he ill?' asked her mother when she came in.

Susie shook her head. 'I think he's gone.'

'Gone? He can't have gone. Have you upset him, Susie?'

'It wasn't me,' said Susie.

Somehow she kept expecting him to come back. The next morning, Sunday, she woke early and listened for the sound of buckets in the yard, but all was silent. She got up and went to do the feeds, looking around all the time. Reuben had come so quietly before that he might come back and she wouldn't even know. But he didn't come. By the end of the day she knew he wouldn't return.

'We'll have to find him,' said Mrs Diamond. 'He's entered for the event next month. I didn't tell him in case he got nervous. It's very hard to get a place in a novice event with an unknown horse, we can't let it go. He has to come back and ride Diamond Bright.'

'Perhaps he'll come back for Doris,' said Susie.

Mrs Diamond made a face. 'Doris! No one would go anywhere for her!'

They supposed that they would slip back into their old, before-Reuben routine. But as the days passed they realized how much they had come to depend on Reuben. Every morning he had risen without complaining, with never a morning off. Every evening he had been last in the yard, making sure all the horses had eaten up and were safely bedded down for the night. Now it was Susie in the mornings once again and Mrs Diamond last thing at night, and both of them were soon weary and short tempered. Susie's schoolwork started to suffer, and she was told off in French and again in Maths. Susie felt tired all the time, and nervous, as if something dreadful was going to happen. But the dreadful thing had happened already. Reuben was gone.

When the weekends came it was worse. Mrs Diamond had asked several people if they knew anyone who could ride Diamond Bright in the event, and one after another they came to try. It was a disaster. Tall, confident girls, big strapping boys, and short gnarled people who looked as if they had been born riding horses, they all came and they all went away again. Diamond had a look, Susie realized, part fright and part wickedness. When that look came into his eye you knew you were in for trouble.

He usually waited until he was at the far end of the field, jumping stickily so the rider was unsettled. He would dodge right, then left, put his back end up and drop his shoulder. If that didn't finish them he would rear.

'He's never reared in his life before,' Mrs Diamond would say distractedly. 'I promise you—'

'He's not ready to event,' said one man.

'He's too wild,' said another.

And a girl, frightened and bruised, said, 'Someone's upset that horse! You should be ashamed to own him. He's dangerous!'

How they wished Reuben would come back. But he was gone and there was no way they could reach him. They had no address, and he might or might not be local. He had come out of nowhere and gone back to it, leaving no trace that he had ever been there at all.

'We can't try any more riders,' said Mrs Diamond one evening. 'They're making the horse worse. Reuben understood him, he likes to be settled, to know where he is with people. All this chopping and changing could ruin him for ever. We'll just have to scratch him from the event.'

Susie put a hand on her mother's arm. 'Not yet. Wait till the last moment. Reuben may come back.'

Her mother smiled sadly.

The time rushed by in busy activity. The worst of it was, thought Susie, there was so little time to ride

Doris. She had become used to coming home from school and going to see the mare. Sometimes she didn't even saddle her, and just slid on to her warm, wide back. Dear Doris. If you brought her a treat she was always pleased to see you, and if you didn't she was only a little disappointed. She did what you asked because she wanted to oblige, because that was the horse she was. Sometimes, ambling down the lanes, between hedges bright with new leaves and the birds darting busily through the air around them, Susie felt happier than she had felt in ages. Everything was fine when she was riding Doris. It was exactly the opposite of Diamond Bright. With him, the problems started the moment you got on!

One Saturday Susie determinedly made time to ride Doris. She rushed to the field after lunch, when the liveries were all eating pie and chips at the pub or sandwiches in the barn, when she should have been eating her own lunch and then cleaning tack. She put the bridle on hastily and climbed on Doris's hairy back. Doris mumbled her bit, wondering why there was such a hurry.

Then Susie realized she had forgotten to open the gate. What's more, riding bareback as she was, if she got off to open it she would have trouble getting back on. She usually mounted at the fence, where there was a good strong bar to stand on. If she stood on the tumbledown gate it would certainly break, and that was another job no one had time for.

The idea came like a little spark of light. 'Why don't we jump the gate?' whispered Susie to the mare.

Doris waggled her huge, grey ears.

'We could,' said Susie softly. 'You can jump anything, Doris!'

The horse blew down her nose just as if she was saying, 'So I can!' and without another thought Susie set her in a brisk canter.

As they neared the gate she felt suddenly doubtful. This wasn't three foot high – it was nearer three foot six! The fence she had jumped before was much smaller. But they were going fast now, and Susie had decided. In an instant there was no turning back. She sat down on Doris's wide body, squeezed with her legs and waited for the shuddering stop.

It didn't come. The mare rose joyously into the air, clearing the gate easily, giving her hind hooves a little flick to keep them out of the way of the fence. She landed with a strong onward roll, and suddenly, with no saddle, Susie knew she would fall off. She stayed on for one stride, and then her knees lost their grip on Doris's rough coat. She slid forward, over Doris's shoulder, and because she couldn't bear to pull on the mare's mouth, let go of the reins. She fell to the ground with a thud.

Doris put down her head and whickered at Susie. Her big feet stamped on the ground anxiously, and her eyelashes batted up and down.

Susie laughed and got to her feet. 'It's all right, old girl,' she said. 'I'm not hurt. No need to get in a state.'

So Doris did get upset when people fell off, she thought, standing on a stone to scramble back on. That was what Reuben had meant.

'You're the best horse ever, Doris,' she said loudly.

'If people don't see how good you are then that's their fault. You're wonderful!'

She turned away from the bridle path and rode through the yard, which her mother had expressly forbidden.

Mrs Diamond saw her and shouted, 'Susie! Don't you dare bring that nag in here!'

'She is not a nag,' said Susie. 'She's a wonderful horse. And I'm riding her in the event next month.'

Mrs Diamond's mouth fell open. 'You will do no such thing!' she exploded, when she found her breath.

'I won't ride anything else,' said Susie. 'We won't be able to do the cross-country within the time, but we'll jump round. And Doris can do the dressage, and the show-jumping. Please, Mum, do say we can! Nobody but Reuben can ride Diamond Bright so instead of Diamond we'll enter Doris. Please!'

Mrs Diamond closed her eyes for a moment. Susie knew she was going to say no. After all, they were entering Diamond because they wanted to sell him, but Doris wasn't even theirs to sell. It would be for nothing.

Just then Mr Barnstaple came out of Major's box. He looked tousled and red faced, as everyone did when they'd been riding Major. All the same, he seemed pleased with himself. When he saw Susie and Doris he said, 'Hello, Susie! Nice to see you riding. Your mother said you'd given up, and here you are on a pretty grey pony. Isn't she nice?'

'Doris is anything but pretty,' said Mrs Diamond,

which showed she was upset. She never contradicted Mr Barnstaple.

'Isn't she?' Mr Barnstaple looked surprised. 'I suppose you're right,' he admitted after a moment. 'But she's got such a kind expression I thought she was. And Susie looks so good up there, no saddle or anything. A positive centaur.'

'Doris is going in next month's novice event,' said Susie boldly. 'It was to be Diamond Bright, but now it's Doris.'

Mrs Diamond glared behind his back. Susie kept her face straight and talked politely to Mr Barnstaple, who said he'd be sure to come and see her. In fact, he'd bring a party of friends. Perhaps they'd allow him to bring a picnic lunch, and entertain them?

'How kind. How lovely,' said Mrs Diamond in a stiff, unnatural voice. Susie knew she was torn between wanting Mr Barnstaple to come with his friends, and hating them all to see Doris. It made her want to laugh.

'Doris is going to do wonderfully,' said Susie. 'Goodbye, Mr Barnstaple.' She turned and rode out of the yard.

Susie and her mother argued every morning after that. 'We should scratch,' insisted Mrs Diamond. 'You're going to make a fool of us all! Who can imagine going into an event with a horse like Doris? Everyone will be there. Everyone I know. Some of the best riders in the country will be bringing their good young horses and we're bringing – that!'

She pointed a quivering finger out of the window.

Doris was in a box now, being pampered. The event was only one day, but a horse had to be fit. Susie was getting up at five in the morning and riding for an hour, and coming back from school and riding again at night, and in between Mrs Diamond had to make sure that Doris was groomed and strapped and trimmed and fussed over, and fed pounds and pounds of oats.

About a week before the event Susie paused while gobbling toast and said, 'Could you watch my dressage test tonight, please? We could do with some help.'

'That horse is beyond help,' said Mrs Diamond. 'Why are we going through all this work and expense and worry, for nothing? We can't sell the horse. Susie, why?'

'We just are,' said Susie. 'It's important.' She wiped her buttery fingers on a tea towel and picked up her bag. If she didn't run she would miss the bus.

'But why is it important?' Her mother was following her to the door.

Susie stopped suddenly. Reuben had said it didn't matter what her mother thought, but it did. She ought to know why. She turned and faced her mother. 'It's important because I'm scared,' she said. 'Even on Doris, I'm scared. And perhaps after this — I won't be.'

She opened the door and raced off across the yard.

Mrs Diamond called, 'Susie—' but the girl didn't wait. She stood watching her tall, red-haired daughter until she was out of sight.

That evening, when Susie got home, she found

Doris tacked up and shining. Her mane had been plaited and her tail neatly pulled, and her big round feet were gleaming with oil. She looked as good as she would ever look, thought Susie.

'Doris, you're beautiful,' she said, because even an ugly horse likes compliments.

'I thought she needed all the help she could get,' said Mrs Diamond, emerging from the tack room. 'Go and get changed, Susie, and we'll run through your test.'

Susie pulled on clean jodhpurs instead of her old darned pair, and found a pair of matching gloves. Her jacket was too tight, but it would have to do. She bundled her hair into a net and crammed her hat on top.

'Right,' said Mrs Diamond, when they entered the ring. 'Pretend this is the real test. I want concentration, accuracy and good presentation. Off you go.'

Susie began. At first it was hard to relax and everything felt lumpy and wrong. Even ordinary trot seemed difficult. But gradually she sat deep in the saddle, lengthened her legs, and felt the horse gather underneath her. After all, it wasn't as if either of them was a beginner. Susie had spent years being taught by her mother, trying to get this or that hard-mouthed pony into extended trot. But she didn't think of that, she didn't think of anything except squeezing with her legs and feeling the reins with her hands, willing Doris to stretch out her legs and pretend she was a thoroughbred.

Mrs Diamond said nothing at all. The final movement was a circle in canter, transition to trot and then halt, horse and rider to leave the ring on a loose rein. The silence continued until Susie was almost out of the arena altogether, and at last Mrs Diamond said, 'Well. That – wasn't bad.'

'We didn't start well,' said Susie.

Her mother nodded. 'You were both nervous. But I'll say this for Doris, she does try for you. Once you began real work she buckled down and did her best.' She glanced down at her marker board and sighed. 'The extended trot's the problem. A horse like this hasn't got the right action. Whatever she does, she's trying to move buckets on the ends of her legs, and other horses have eggcups. Still, we can but try. I must admit, Susie, when it comes to dressage you leave Reuben Black standing. Take her round in trot.'

Susie grinned to herself. If there was one thing her mother couldn't resist it was a challenge. She ran a hand quickly over Doris's shining neck. Good old Doris.

'Keep your hand *on* the rein, Susie!' yelled her mother. 'How can you expect a horse to concentrate when you mess her about? Let's have our aids *clear* and *positive*, shall we? The horse is doing her best and so must you!'

Susie began to chuckle, and every step the horse took made her laugh more. It was just as always. Riding Doris made her so, so happy.

Chapter Eight

On the day of the event they left the yard very early in the morning. The horses left behind put their heads over their doors to watch so much bustle in the half light of dawn, and Diamond Bright called out with a hopeful whicker.

'You can keep quiet,' said Mrs Diamond, wagging a finger at him. 'This should have been you. What a bad horse you are.'

Diamond put up his ears and called again. He looked the picture of innocence. Nobody would guess he was such a rogue.

Doris, still yawning, walked obligingly into the wagon, and all at once Susie felt her heart sink. She was such a small, ugly, ordinary horse in such a shabby wagon. When they led her out at the event there would be dozens and dozens of beautiful horses, looking down their long noses at humble little Doris, who should know better than to have ideas beyond her station. It was like taking a horse that pulled a rag and bone cart and making it run in the Derby, thought Susie.

Mrs Diamond said, 'Come on, Susie!' and hustled

by with a wicker basket full of rugs and extra tack.

Susie turned to her. 'Doris isn't the right sort of horse. Everyone will laugh.'

Her mother put the basket in the wagon just the same. 'I daresay they will,' she said. 'But we shall surprise them. Don't hang about thinking, Susie, it only makes it worse. You worry far too much.'

But what else was there to do but worry? The sun came up as the wagon pulled out of the yard, lighting the sky with a glorious blaze of pink and violet and golden-tinged grey. A baby rabbit hopped along the lane in front of them, and Susie thought, if only I wasn't going to the event I could enjoy this lovely morning. Her stomach was tight with panic, her fingers felt numb and lifeless, and yet she didn't know why she was afraid. It was as if she knew that something terrible was going to happen, something much worse than all the things that might happen. She could make a fool of herself in the dressage test and be laughed out of the ring; she could fall off at a water jump and everyone would see; she could end up in an ambulance with a broken leg. But the fear was bigger than all that. It wasn't about anything, she realized. It was just fear.

If only your body could leave the fear behind, she thought. If only you could come back for it later. But it was like chains hanging on to your arms and legs, stopping you doing anything well. She had to shake the chains off. She had to shake and shake until they flew right away, and she was like everyone else, free.

Mrs Diamond glanced at her daughter's white face. 'Everyone's nervous before events,' she said cheerfully.

But Susie knew this wasn't just nerves. It was as if she was riding Diamond and Major and that nasty pony she had been given when she was ten because the girl who owned it couldn't ride it, and they were all rolled up in one rearing, bolting, biting package called Doris. Perhaps that was Doris, she thought. Perhaps Doris would be like that at an event.

She knelt on the seat and looked back into the wagon. And Doris was there. Dear, dependable Doris, with her long eyelashes and her big, kind face. She wasn't a monster, just a horse. Susie could only be laughed at or break a leg.

'I hope I don't break a leg,' she said to her mother.

'You mustn't think about things like that,' said her mother bracingly.

But Susie could think about nothing else. She was sure she was going to break a leg!

To Susie's surprise, Mr Barnstaple was already there when they arrived. He didn't know much about these horsey things, he said, but he'd found them a good place to park, and he had a flask of coffee and would Susie like some cherry cake to settle her down? Susie didn't want anything but it seemed rude to refuse, and when she'd eaten she felt better.

She walked the course and every fence looked like a mountain. It was consoling, though, to hear other riders saying the same. One girl stood at the water jump where the course photographers were setting up their equipment and said, 'I'll never get through this. He hates water. If someone takes a picture of me falling in I shall die!'

Her dressage test was in half an hour. She went to get her number while her mother got Doris ready, and suddenly it was all a rush.

'Put your hair in the net, Susie!' Mrs Diamond instructed. 'Remember, look confident and calm.'

'I think she looks rather elegant,' said Mr Barnstaple, trying to cheer everyone up. 'Love the hairnet, Susie!'

'Do be quiet, Tom,' said Mrs Diamond distractedly. 'Susie has to concentrate.'

Mr Barnstaple obediently shut up.

Once she was on the horse, Susie should have felt better, but she didn't. She rode down between the lines of horse wagons, and a girl with a huge bay gelding hid a laugh behind her hand. Susie imagined everyone laughing, looking at her, all done up, on a rag and bone pony. Her mother was hobbling along behind, and she imagined everyone laughing at her, too, so lame and still so determined. Suddenly she felt angry. Let them laugh, she thought. We'll show them. She shortened her reins and asked Doris to trot, willing her to point her heavy toe. Doris bent her head and clumped across the grass, snorting the air on this fine spring morning. It was a lovely day, Susie remembered. Doris was really pleased with it.

They watched the test just before theirs. It looked brilliant. A girl on a chestnut sailed through the movements as if dancing on water, and Susie's heart sank to her boots and then into the floor, and then further still, if that was possible.

Mrs Diamond said, 'I do not like the way that horse holds its head. They're bound to mark it down.'

'Absolutely,' said Mr Barnstaple. 'Dreadful exhibition.'

Susie wished they would go away and not watch. When she made a mess of it they would be so terribly kind. Oh, dear, she thought, as the chestnut left the ring. Oh, oh, dear.

The klaxon sounded for the next competitor. Susie did nothing at all.

'Go on, Susie!' said Mrs Diamond.

'Go on, Susie!' echoed Mr Barnstaple. 'You show 'em. Deep breath. Head up. Off you go!'

There was no way out of this now. If she turned back it would be worse than going on. Susie squeezed her legs against Doris's sides and started into the ring. Her mind went off in strange thoughts. Did people feel like this when they were going to the guillotine? They couldn't feel worse. And this was just a dressage test! Centre of the ring. Good halt. Bow. Look at those judges, nobody's laughing. How they do stare.

And then it was over. Where had the moments gone? Susie rode out of the ring, blinking in the sunshine, and her mother said, 'Well done, Susie! And well done, Doris! That mare really does rise to the occasion.'

'Was it all right?' asked Susie.

'Brilliant. Brilliant!' said Mr Barnstaple, who of course knew nothing about it.

'Creditable,' said Mrs Diamond. 'And remarkable for a horse like Doris. I see I've taught you something in all these years, Susie. I take all the credit.'

That made Susie laugh. She slipped off Doris and gave her a drink.

They had an hour to wait before the cross-country, and Doris needed bandages and grease to protect her legs, and Mrs Diamond's jumping saddle, and the old bridle with the non-slip reins. All the smart gear was bundled back into the wagon, and Susie pulled on an ordinary pair of jodhpurs, a yellow jumper and a jockey skull with a black and yellow silk.

'I wore these when I evented,' said Mrs Diamond cheerfully. 'I always thought they brought me luck.'

Susie shuddered. She could do without her mother's luck. Mr Barnstaple's friends had begun to arrive, and somebody opened some champagne and poured glasses for everyone. It was like a party when you're the only person who hasn't been invited, thought Susie. Mr Barnstaple poured some champagne into a paper cup and made her take a sip. 'Dutch courage,' he said.

'Susie isn't afraid,' said Mrs Diamond sharply.

And oddly enough, she wasn't so much. Everywhere about her, highly strung horses were snorting and bucking and behaving badly, while Doris quietly blinked.

One girl suddenly yelled, 'I'm going to be sick!' and was, in her horse's water bucket. Her mother was furious. She sent the girl across to borrow another bucket, and Susie said, 'I go in twenty minutes.'

The girl made a face. 'I've got two hours to wait!

I'll have died by then!' And she staggered off, still looking dreadful.

At the start, even Mrs Diamond felt the strain. She kept telling Susie which jumps to take slowly and which to tackle with speed, and it all seemed a terrible muddle. Everything was going quiet again, as if she wasn't really there, and the starter was making faces and smiling, and counting down on his big electric watch. Any moment now. Come on, Doris. Don't let me down. Doris, come on!

They were away in a good steady gallop. The first jump was a log and Doris hopped it, turning at once to the double of gates at the bottom of the hill. Susie collected her and Doris was neat, one quick stride between the two elements. On, up the hill, with a brush fence at the top and a drop further on. One by one the fences went, each so much smaller than they had seemed when they walked the course. Doris was going well, enjoying herself, turning happily down to the water. If I get wet, thought Susie, I don't care. It's worth it!

But Doris slowed at the water's edge, popped happily in, gathered her big square hocks under her and jumped out. All the spectators clapped.

As they came up to the finish Susie knew they were over the time. The mare was blowing hard, and she let her come back to a steady canter. As she drew up a great cheer went up from Mr Barnstaple and his friends, and Mrs Diamond, eyes shining with delight, said, 'Susie, that was wonderful! Absolutely wonderful!'

Susie slipped off the horse, unfastening the saddle to go and weigh in. She saw someone out of the corner of her eye. It was only a glimpse before she was in the tent, and the clerk of the scales was saying, 'Bet you're glad that's done, young lady!' and when she came out he was gone. But she had seen him. Reuben's friend. Danny.

The showjumping didn't begin until late in the afternoon. They washed Doris off and gave her a feed, and she dozed contentedly in the sunshine, a few oats hanging on her lips. She didn't look at all the sort of horse that could compete in an event! The commentary kept reporting falls and refusals, as one by one all the young horses made mistakes. One of Mr Barnstaple's friends went to look at the score board and said they were lying fifth, with still a lot of people to go, and Susie was seized with a fit of the giggles. Fifth! Doris! Her!

An enormous picnic lunch had been laid out on a cloth on the grass. Susie ate some pork pie, a hardboiled egg and some crisps, but that was enough. She felt very tired suddenly, and rather thirsty, so she drank a lot of lemonade. Everyone was talking and Mr Barnstaple was making her mother laugh, so she got up and wandered away through the horse boxes, back towards the place she had seen Danny.

Faces were everywhere, dogs, children, men in motorbike helmets, but no Danny. Susie kept on walking, down the lines of tents selling horsey things and country clothing, and hot dogs and sweets and beer. Sometimes she glimpsed a brown jacket and sometimes a sharp face, but it was never Danny. She turned back to the horse boxes. And there he was. Watching her.

'Hello,' she said. 'You're Danny, aren't you? Reuben's friend.'

He didn't say anything. He had black hair and dark skin, with a scarf tied round his throat. He looked like Reuben when he first came. A gypsy.

'Thank you for Doris,' said Susie. 'She's wonderful. Did you see?'

He nodded. 'Always goes well, does Doris.'

'It should have been Diamond Bright,' said Susie. 'No one can ride him except Reuben. I wish you'd tell me where he is. I want to ask him to come back.'

Danny looked about him, at the crowds with their dogs and their money. 'Reuben don't fit in here.'

'Yes he does! If you can ride you fit in. And Reuben can. He could be an event rider, a jockey, anything. Please make him come back, if he doesn't then I don't know what's going to happen to Diamond Bright. The horse is going bad, no one can ride him, and if Reuben doesn't come back then he'll have to be shot!'

Danny's eyes widened in horror. 'Can't shoot a good horse,' he said.

'Well, we're going to,' Susie insisted, although she couldn't possibly imagine anyone shooting Diamond Bright. 'You must tell me where Reuben is at once.'

'Best if I take you,' said Danny. 'Tomorrow morning. Early.'

Susie opened her mouth to ask where they were

going, but it was too late. Danny had melted into the crowd. He was the sort of person you only found if they wanted you to find them, she thought. Like Reuben. They weren't as well behaved and ordinary as everyone else. A little bit of the wild was still with them.

She went back to the wagon and moved Doris into the shade. Mrs Diamond had bought her some ice-cream and she leaned against the wheel of the wagon and ate it fast before it melted. Suddenly she thought that she didn't care at all how the showjumping went. Doris could knock everything down twice over and be eliminated. Whatever happened next, this would still be a truly wonderful day.

Chapter Nine

Susie set her alarm for five o'clock the next morning, and when it went off she thought it must still be the middle of the night. She lay in the dark for a few moments, wondering if Danny might not come. She was so tired! Yesterday had been the most wonderful and exciting day of her whole life and she would give anything to lie here in bed and dream about it. Sixth! Sixth in her first event.

Diamond would have won it, she thought, and sat up. Diamond would have shown the world what a great horse he was. She got out of bed and scrambled into jeans and jumper, dragging a brush through her tousled red hair.

Early as she was, Danny was earlier. He appeared out of the gloom like a ghost, and Susie jumped.

'Come on,' he said, and melted towards the field gate. Susie followed, wondering where they were going, and saw that they were cutting across the meadow to the road. A van was parked there, where it wouldn't be seen, and Danny motioned to her to get in.

As she opened the van door she heard a low growl. She took in her breath, sharply.

'Only the dog,' said Danny. 'He's a lurcher.'

Susie peered into the gloom behind the seats and saw a huge, brindled dog with bright eyes. The bodies of four or five rabbits were hung up next to him, and Susie opened her mouth to say something and then closed it again. She got into the car.

'Get you a lurcher pup if you want,' said Danny.

'Would you?'

'Keep themselves, lurchers. But the keepers catch you if you don't train them right.'

'How do you train them?' Susie glanced over her shoulder at the dog, who had decided she was a friend and was wagging his tail.

'Need them used to ferrets, that's one thing.' He motioned to a box by Susie's feet. 'Go on, have a look. Good hob ferret, that is.'

She lifted the lid and peered in. A sandy, triangular face peeped out at her, full of teeth, and she shut the lid again, quickly. 'Is that all they need to know?'

'Best if you teach them "come here",' said Danny. 'But it don't mean "come here". When I tell him "come here" he takes himself off, and no one can say he's my dog. Won't come, will he? Best way when the keeper's about.'

Susie laughed. She liked Danny, and he was a lot more talkative than Reuben.

They took so many twisting back lanes that Susie soon lost her bearings. The dawn was touching the sky with purple light, and all the creatures of the hedgerows were busy hiding themselves again, ready for the day.

'I thought Reuben had gone back to the council house,' said Susie.

Danny snorted. 'Not him. Kill him, it would, to leave the horses. Never been no good at nothing else, him.'

After half an hour or so they came to a green ride between hedges, and Danny stopped the van and got out. He whistled, piercingly, and set off across the grass. Susie followed close behind. There, by the hedge was a small gypsy caravan, with three ponies grazing near by. Some hens were pecking the ground roundabout, and a big, grey lurcher stood up as they approached and warned them off.

'Is Reuben here?' asked Susie.

And a voice behind her said, 'Aye.'

She spun round. He was looking cross and wary. His hair needed cutting and he was wearing his old clothes, the ones that no longer fitted. She thought of all the bags and parcels waiting in his flat for his return.

'Danny said you was going to shoot Diamond,' said Reuben. 'I know that ain't true.'

Susie shrugged. 'There isn't anything else you can do with a horse no one can ride.'

'You can find someone. Takes a bit of time, that's all.'

'We've tried loads of people! He's going from bad to worse, Reuben. Soon he'll really hurt someone and then he will have to be shot. Truly.'

He looked more sullen than ever, and she could see he was turning it over in his mind.

She said, 'Can I look in the caravan?' and before he could say no she climbed the steps and looked inside.

It was bare and clean, with a wood stove in one corner and a bed in the other. A little pile of books and papers stood on the floor, and Susie whirled round, saying, 'I knew you'd keep on with the reading! I bet you're really good by now.'

'Get out of there.' Reuben came across and pulled the canvas curtain down in front of his home. He glared at Susie, and went across to see to his ponies. Gypsy ponies all of them, one big cob and a couple of skewbalds.

'I came sixth in the event with Doris,' said Susie. 'We were over time in the cross-country. I'm still scared, but not nearly as bad.'

'You ride Diamond, then,' said Reuben. 'Why don't you?'

'Oh, ha ha,' said Susie. 'Shall I ask my mother to give you more money? I know she would. She's desperate.'

Reuben said nothing, but busied himself altering a headcollar that was perfectly all right. 'You friends with that girl again?' he asked.

Susie shrugged. 'Ellen? Yes. But not the same. And I shut Naomi up. I went back and stuck a Big Mac in her hair.'

Reuben's eyes widened. 'You didn't!'

Susie nodded. 'She smelled of mayonnaise for a week.'

He laughed then, in real amusement. 'Have to bring these,' he said, jerking a thumb at the ponies. 'And the dog.'

'Oh,' said Susie. She knew what her mother would think of that.

'Best be getting back, then,' said Reuben.

'Will you come today?' asked Susie.

He shrugged, but she knew that he would.

It was barely eight o'clock by the time she got home. Her mother was working in the yard. 'Did you go for a walk?' she asked. 'I thought you'd have a lie-in this morning. You've earned it.'

'I went to see Reuben,' said Susie. 'He's coming back. With three horses and a lurcher.'

Mrs Diamond's mouth opened and closed. At last she said, 'Well. Are we to be overrun with gypsy ponies? Are we to be the gypsy-pony stables of the country? Should I get rid of anything with a hint of quality, sell it all, everything, and fill the boxes with scrubby ponies and lurcher dogs?'

'He's going to ride Diamond Bright,' said Susie. 'So it's going to be worth it.'

Her mother sighed. 'I hope it isn't too late. That horse is impossible nowadays. Perhaps even Reuben can't ride him.'

'You don't mind that I said he could come?'

'I don't know,' said Mrs Diamond. For a moment she looked very bleak. 'Wages to pay, and more horses to feed, and a dog. But we do need Reuben. I suppose we'll manage somehow.'

He arrived on foot in the afternoon, the three ponies trailing after him on long ropes, the dog trotting by the hedge. When Susie came out to meet them, Reuben said to the dog, 'Get back!' and the animal trotted up, wagging its tail.

'So Danny was telling the truth!' said Susie. 'What have you done with the caravan?'

'Never you mind,' said Reuben.

He was casting a critical eye round the yard, and Susie could tell he thought they had let things get into a mess again. She flicked her fingers at the dog. 'Get back! Get back!' she said, and the dog stepped delicately forward. He had a long, gentle face with huge brown eyes.

'You'll make him soft, petting,' said Reuben. 'Give over, Flash.'

The horses went in Doris's old field, and kicked up their heels to be off tethers. Reuben watched them for a moment, then turned away.

'Right,' he said. 'Let's be seeing him, then.'

'Who?'

'Diamond, of course.'

The horse was turned out during the day in the meadow close to the house. Mrs Diamond liked to look out from her kitchen window and see him. Susie didn't like looking at him at all. He made her feel sad. A beautiful, spirited horse was being wasted. When she leaned on the fence and called to him he cantered across the grass with a beautiful, flowing stride, which turned into a high-stepping prance as he came up to them.

'You don't change none,' said Reuben.

Diamond blew down his nose, and then as Susie put out a hand he danced away, only to come back again a few moments later.

'Getting above yourself, I see,' said Reuben.

'He's always been above himself,' said Susie. 'When he's in a mood like this we can never catch him. But isn't he beautiful?'

'Nowt beautiful about a useless horse,' said Reuben, and vaulted over the fence and into the paddock.

He stamped straight up to Diamond, pulled his belt from his jeans and looped it round the horse's neck. Diamond snorted in surprise. He hadn't meant to be caught. He wasn't expecting it. 'Get on in, you ____,' said Reuben. Diamond did as he was told.

But they were all nervous about riding Diamond Bright. Susie and Mrs Diamond had seen too many hopefuls bucked off, jumped off and run away with and their apprehension even affected Reuben.

'The horse has got too clever,' explained Mrs Diamond. 'He has his little tricks.'

'He drops his shoulder sometimes,' said Susie. 'That gets rid of loads of people.'

'And he overjumps,' added her mother. 'When he does that and bucks, everyone flies off.'

Reuben went to get his hat. Then he went into the tack room and came out carrying a large, heavy stick.

'He hates sticks,' said Mrs Diamond. 'We've tried hitting him and I warn you—'

'I ain't going to hit him,' said Reuben. 'Frighten him, just, and he don't frighten easy, that horse. I'll borrow them leather things you wear, Susie.'

'My chaps?' Susie blinked. She liked her chaps,

they made her feel like a cowboy. 'Oh. All right.'

The big, leather flaps fastened round Reuben's waist and laced around his legs. But he left the lower part flapping, in a way that was sure to frighten the horse. No one said anything. After all, they weren't riding. The lurcher, Flash, pushed his head under Susie's hand, as if for comfort. Reuben led Diamond Bright into the field and mounted.

The horse was quivering with excitement. Reuben settled in the saddle, the chaps flapping in the breeze. Underneath him Diamond Bright seemed like a spring, coiled tight and about to explode into action. Reuben gathered his reins and squeezed with his legs, but for a long, long second the horse remained quite still.

Then, with a high-pitched squeal, Diamond flung himself into a gallop. He travelled no more than ten yards before Reuben stopped him, whirled him around and slammed the stick down on to the flapping leather of his chaps. It made a loud 'Thwack!' and Diamond shuddered to a halt. 'Now,' said Reuben to himself. 'Now.' He squeezed with his legs again. This time Diamond trotted four strides, then plunged sideways. By some miracle Reuben stayed on, although he lost a stirrup. Again he lifted the stick and again crashed it down not on the horse, but on leather. Diamond Bright's ears swivelled as far as they could go. What was this noise? Where was it coming from? He hadn't been struck and he didn't understand.

For the third time Reuben asked the horse to walk

on. This time it worked. They made almost a full circuit of the paddock before Diamond lunged forward and was stopped. Again the stick thwacked down noisily, although the horse felt nothing at all. Soon Reuben could circle the paddock at walk and trot just as he wished.

Mrs Diamond made a face at Susie. 'Well,' she said. 'That boy certainly knows a thing or two. He's got that horse puzzled enough to behave at last.'

But it wasn't the end of the struggle. Diamond was a clever horse who had become used to getting his own way. What worked on him one day didn't work the next. It was almost as if he stood in his stable all night plotting some new mischief, and Reuben had to plot just as hard to outwit him. He would buck and rear and dive sideways under trees, and twice Reuben fell off. But Diamond didn't gallop away. It was almost as if he was enjoying the battle, and hated Reuben to lose. When he got back on Diamond behaved a little better for a while.

One day, when Reuben was grooming Diamond, Susie leaned on the door of the box. 'I don't know why you bother,' she said. 'You do so much for him and he's so naughty.'

Reuben grunted. For a moment Susie thought he was in one of his silent moods, but suddenly he said, 'Feels good, when we get it right. He likes it just as much. Can hear him thinking, I can. Daresay he can hear me.'

'Is that because you're a gypsy? I mean – a traveller?'

He shrugged. 'Dunno. Shouldn't think so. Anyone can hear a horse thinking if they listen hard enough. You can hear Doris, can't you?'

Susie considered. 'Sometimes I know what she's going to do,' she admitted. 'But that's just knowing her well, isn't it?'

'You know a horse well enough and you can hear him thinking,' Reuben repeated, and went back to his work.

It didn't take long for the news of Reuben's return to spread. One morning Susie went into school and found a huge heart drawn on the blackboard and the words 'Susie loves a dirty gypsy' written in it. Naomi Fisher. It had to be. She looked accusingly at Ellen, who could have rubbed it out but was pretending to do her homework instead. Everyone was watching, waiting to see what she would do. Naomi was grinning, sure Susie would have to rub it out. Susie forced a smile to her lips and went to her desk, leaving the heart for all to see.

It was still there when Miss Parker came in for registration. She looked at the heart, and then at Susie. 'What is all this about, Susie?' she asked sharply.

Susie looked up. 'I don't know, Miss Parker. We've got a gypsy boy working for us at the stables, that's all.'

Miss Parker's face became stern. 'I will not have such prejudice in my class!' she declared. 'Who wrote this? Whoever it is had better own up at once and explain themselves. Good and bad people come in all colours and all shapes and sizes, and I won't have someone victimized over something as trivial as giving a job to a gypsy. Now, unless someone admits to this silly behaviour you will all stay in after school. All except you, Susie,' she added.

At break the whole class told Naomi she should own up. But nothing they could say would make her. All day no one thought about anything else, and when half past three came the only person going home was Susie. She almost wished she was staying too.

'You should have rubbed it out,' said Ellen.

'I didn't write it,' said Susie. 'Anyway, you could have rubbed it out too.'

'Stupid Naomi shouldn't have written it in the first place,' said Ellen.

It was a sentiment the whole class agreed with. Naomi sat in her place, silent and angry. Suddenly she lifted her head, giving Susie a furious stare. 'I'll get even with you, Susie Diamond,' she said.

Chapter Ten

It was hard to know what to do with Diamond Bright. Reuben wanted to enter him in an event, but Mrs Diamond had her doubts. She knew the standards expected, and Diamond was still quite likely to leap out of the dressage arena at a moment's notice. He wasn't at all reliable.

'Give him something to think on,' Reuben insisted. 'Horse like that gets bored with same old stuff. Needs to use his brain.'

Mrs Diamond lost her temper. 'If you used your brain, Reuben, you'd realize we'd probably make an exhibition of ourselves *and* ruin the horse. The best we can hope for now is to get him rideable and sell him to someone who can give him time.'

'Throwing money away, that is,' insisted Reuben. 'Top class horse you got here.'

'In five years' time, he might be,' agreed Mrs Diamond. 'We haven't got five years! If you knew how much it costs to run this place, and how little we make—' She bit her lip and turned away. Sometimes she forgot that Reuben wasn't one of the family. She told him more than she should.

That evening Reuben waited for Susie off the

school bus. She got off slowly, feeling herself going red. Now everyone would really talk.

'What's the matter?' she asked crossly. 'What are you doing here?'

Reuben didn't seem to notice she was upset. 'Got to talk to your mum,' he said. 'Make her see sense. Diamond's got to go in one of them event things. We're all ready, him and me.'

Susie laughed unkindly. 'You are not! He can't do a good dressage test to save his life, he bucks like crazy!'

'He only does that at home.'

'You can't know that. It's only what you think.'

'I know what I think.' Reuben was grim and determined.

Susie turned the thought over in her mind. But Diamond Bright was so unpredictable. Her mother was right about him, he was too young and his temperament was wrong. The stable had a reputation to keep up, and horses like Diamond Bright would do it less good even than horses like Doris. Besides, Susie was cross with Reuben. She didn't want to back him up.

She said, 'The fact is, Reuben, Diamond Bright's not ready. He may never be ready, you've tried your best and he's still wild. No event's going to cure that. You'll just have to accept it.'

She walked off, glancing back over her shoulder to see Reuben watching her with angry eyes.

But the very next day a letter came from the bank.

Susie's mother read it in silence, the colour draining from her face. Then she sat down suddenly and clenched her hands together.

'We've got to sell up,' she said in a quiet, rather shaky voice. 'We owe the bank so much money that they say we have to sell the house, the horses, everything.'

Susie tried to speak, but her voice had gone. Her mother's words seemed to make no sense. Sell? Sell her home? She had been born here, she had lived here all her life. All her memories, of Daddy and the ponies, everything, had all been centred on this house, these fields, the horses. 'We can't,' she said croakily.

'Darling, I'm sorry, but we must. I knew it was coming. That's why I was so upset when Diamond Bright turned out so badly. We needed him to be a success and he was such a disappointment. Oh Susie, I'm sorry I've let you down. I'm so sorry!'

Susie went out into the fields, to the far meadow, with Flash at her heels. Doris and the gypsy ponies were grazing by the stream, heads down, tails swishing lazily. When Doris saw Susie she ambled across and snuffled at her pockets for treats. Susie found some old pony nuts and fed them to her. Dear Doris. How terrible it would be when there was no Doris in her life, no horses at all. Once she had wanted nothing more to do with them, and now, a life without horses didn't seem like life at all. It would be empty.

As she walked back to the house she saw Reuben

in the ring, working Diamond Bright. She watched for a moment, seeing so many things that were wrong. The horse was stiff into corners, he resisted when asked to bend, his halt was crooked and fidgety. But if he could only show potential in an event, then someone might buy him. He would have to be sold anyway now. She called to Reuben, and Diamond pretended to take fright, shying half across the arena. Susie took no notice and walked across.

'I've changed my mind,' she said tightly. 'I'm going to enter Diamond for the event at the end of the month. I won't tell my mother, and neither must you.'

'What's brought this on?' asked Reuben. He sat on the horse as he always did, a forward slouch in the saddle, like a monkey.

'Never you mind,' said Susie, and walked away.

Somehow it seemed that everything was going wrong at once. School was full of Naomi Fisher and mean tricks, from ink on her books to rude notes stuck on her back that made everyone laugh and Susie feel a fool. At home her mother was silent and miserable, and men kept coming round the stables, valuing things. Even Mr Barnstaple was unhappy, because he would have to find somewhere else for Major. 'No one understands him like your mother, Susie,' he told her one day, looking sadly at the big horse.

Susie took a deep breath. 'You could buy a lot of horses nicer than Major, Mr Barnstaple,' she said. 'He isn't the best horse in the world.'

Mr Barnstaple chuckled. 'I know that,' he said.

'But I'm fond of the old boy. I keep thinking that no one else would put up with him, so I can't sell him to anyone. He bites and he's not very clever, but on his good days he and I have a lot of fun. I don't know a lot about horses but I do know that if you like a horse and he likes you it doesn't matter what anyone else thinks. That's the horse for you.'

'Like me and Doris,' said Susie.

Mr Barnstaple nodded. 'And Reuben and Diamond Bright.'

Susie thought, you didn't have to ride well to understand things. Mr Barnstaple might have a terrible seat, but he was really awfully kind.

But not even Reuben could make Diamond Bright behave himself just then. Susie watched them working in the ring, and twice Diamond took fright at a shadow and bucked. The second time Reuben was bucked off. He got up, trying to look as if it didn't matter, although it did. The horse had been coming to hand nicely, and now he was going mad again.

Susie's eyes narrowed. Diamond had never been fitter, he was a mass of gleaming chestnut muscle. Surely that was the problem.

'You're going to have to let him down,' she shouted. 'You'll never even get him to start the dressage test if he's like this.'

Reuben glanced across. 'He's fit. Got to be fit.'

'But he's too fit. A good event horse has to be calm as well as fit. Turn him out at night, and let him calm down.'

'You telling me how to manage the horse?' demanded Reuben.

Susie nodded fiercely. 'You don't know everything. No one knows everything about horses, and you don't know how to produce an eventer. If you don't turn him out you're going to be in trouble!'

'My trouble. Not yours. I'm not too scared to ride him!'

Susie stormed back to the house. If Reuben wouldn't listen he would make a mess of everything, and it was their very last chance! Diamond Bright had to do well. She pushed open the kitchen door and stood for a moment, smelling the warm, safe smells of her home. Nowhere else would ever be like this. A warm body pressed against her legs and she looked down. It was Flash, the lurcher, close to her heels, trying to sneak into the kitchen to toast his toes by the fire. He always did when he grew tired of waiting for Reuben. Susie wanted to throw him out because he was Reuben's dog and Reuben wouldn't listen, but Flash looked so sad and unhappy at the thought of his cold feet that she couldn't. She was sad and unhappy too. She put her arms around him and he licked the tears from her cheeks.

She went to bed early, and lay awake for what seemed like ages. But she must have slept eventually, because suddenly she found herself jerked awake. She glanced at her clock. It was half past two. Something had woken her.

Susie went to the window and listened. There it was, a dull, solid banging, the sound of a horse in distress. She got out of bed, pulled on boots and a jacket and went downstairs.

It was Diamond. He was pacing his box, stopping now and then to kick at his stomach with his back legs, sometimes turning to bite at himself, sometimes striking out at the wall. Colic. Susie had seen it before. She felt her own insides twisting with alarm. She reached up for Diamond's headcollar, and at that moment Reuben appeared by the door. The noise had woken him too.

'Get my mother,' said Susie urgently. 'He needs a drench. I knew you were doing this horse too well!'

'Saying it's my fault, are you?' demanded Reuben. He looked pale and frightened and very young.

'Colic isn't anyone's fault,' said Susie. 'It just happens. Get my mother while I lead him round.'

At first Diamond didn't want to walk, but Susie coaxed and bullied him. By the time Mrs Diamond came rushing into the yard, her hair on end and her dressing-gown inside out, he was looking a little better.

'I'll drench him,' said Mrs Diamond. 'Cooking oil usually works. You've been keeping him far too fit, Reuben, and feeding him far too well. You should have turned him out.'

She went off to fetch the oil, and Susie made a face at Reuben. 'Told you so.'

He scowled. 'Don't know what's got into you, lately. Right bad mood you're always in.'

Susie said nothing, and kept on walking the horse.

'Let me have him,' said Reuben.

She shook her head. 'He was mine before he was yours.'

'Jealous, are you? Is that all it is?'

'I am not jealous!' To her shame she found tears on her eyelashes and she brushed them away. 'It's just — oh, you wouldn't understand! We're in such trouble.'

He looked as if he was going to ask questions, but to her relief, Mrs Diamond came back with the oil.

'Is he going to die?' asked Reuben fearfully.

Mrs Diamond shook her head. 'I doubt it.'

'We had a horse die once,' said Reuben. 'Twisted gut.'

'I think we caught this in time. It's just indigestion. Hold his head up, Susie, while I drench him.'

Susie forced Diamond's nose skywards. The horse snorted in pain and indignation, and Susie crooned to him soothingly. Mrs Diamond climbed on to the mounting block, a jug of cooking oil in her hand. She reached into Diamond's mouth and took hold of his tongue, pulling it sideways to stop him closing his teeth. Then she poured the oil steadily down the horse's throat, while Diamond's eyes rolled in his head in surprise. When she finished she shook her arm irritably.

'I always get it right down me,' she said. 'Lead him round again, Susie. Reuben can take over when you're tired.'

Susie nodded, and began trudging in a circle again. Diamond Bright was quieter now, and his restless kicking had stopped. He kept making faces at the taste of the cooking oil. But Susie and Reuben kept him moving, hour after hour. Only when dawn was breaking did her mother say they could stop. Diamond hung his head sleepily and Susie and Reuben yawned like horses themselves. They went into the house for breakfast.

Mrs Diamond was cooking bacon and eggs. 'I worry about that horse,' she said as they came in. 'He's got such potential, but if we're not careful he'll never realize it. I wish he had a chance to show what he can do.'

'An event or something,' said Susie.

Her mother nodded. 'Yes. Perhaps I should have entered him. It's too late now.'

'No it ain't,' said Reuben.

Nobody said anything. The noise of frying bacon suddenly seemed very loud.

'Reuben, there's something I've been meaning to tell you,' said Mrs Diamond jerkily. 'It's rather difficult, but – well, you're not going to have a job any more. And the horses have to go. And Susie and I are losing our home. We have to sell up, you see. Everything.'

Reuben looked from Susie to her mother and back again. He nodded. 'Figures,' he said. 'She's been in a right sour mood.'

'I have not!' snapped Susie. 'It's you, behaving as if you're in charge, not taking any advice on how to get Diamond ready!'

'Ready for what?' asked Mrs Diamond.

Susie felt herself growing hot. 'The event,' she said

at last. 'It was all I could think of. If Diamond does well we might sell him and pay off our debts.'

Mrs Diamond looked from Susie to Reuben and back again. 'And this is why Diamond's been jumping out of his skin?'

They both nodded. 'He's a grand horse,' said Reuben. 'Working every day we've been.'

'And Susie was right,' said Mrs Diamond. 'You've got that horse far too fit. From now on, Reuben, I shall give you a lesson every day and I want Diamond in a suitable frame of mind. What can you have been thinking of, not telling me of this before? We've got work to do. Serious work.'

'So you're not angry?' asked Susie in surprise. 'You said we shouldn't do it.'

Her mother put an arm around her shoulders. 'But that was before I knew we were going to have to leave,' she said. 'I couldn't bear to sell Diamond Bright and never see him do well. And if he doesn't do well, at least we'll have tried. I think it's what your father would have wanted. Thank you, Susie, and you too, Reuben. You've done such a lot for us.'

Reuben was blushing. 'Bacon's burning,' he muttered, and sat at the table, even his ears going pink.

Chapter Eleven

As the event drew closer they all began to hope that Diamond Bright would do wonderfully well. It wasn't a sensible hope, of course, because he was a young and inexperienced horse, and wild into the bargain. But they hoped anyway.

It was the only thing that kept them going. Now that they knew the place was closing, one by one the livery owners were taking their horses away to other stables, and one by one Mrs Diamond was selling her own stock. Two broodmares went, one of them Diamond's mother, and a colt they had been planning to break that summer. People came and bought tack and buckets and farm machinery, and took it away with them. Everything began to seem bare and broken down, as if they had already left and all the horses and people were gone. But Doris and the gypsy horses stayed, putting their big heads through the fences, watching the comings and goings in the yard with old, calm eyes.

Mrs Diamond worked and worked on Reuben's dressage. But it seemed the more they worked the worse it became. Diamond Bright had no patience, after half an hour he was restless and wanted to give up. If you persisted he would dance sideways, fidget and in the end buck. He could look like a bronco sometimes, not a dressage horse at all. Reuben was little better. Dressage bored him.

The night before the event Mrs Diamond was pale with anxiety. 'I've made a mess of everything, and now Diamond Bright is going to finish off with the biggest mess of all,' she said to Susie.

'He'll be brilliant at the cross-country,' said Susie determinedly.

'If he doesn't kill Reuben! He's so headstrong. And dressage makes him worse. If he's drawn to go less than an hour after the dressage test he'll be like an unguided missile. I can't let Reuben do it, Susie. Really I can't.'

She got up to go out to the yard. Susie wanted to say something to stop her, but couldn't think of anything that would. She stood at the window and watched her mother talking to Reuben. At first he stood looking sullenly at the floor, but all of a sudden he started waving his arms and talking nineteen to the dozen. She had no need to say anything, Susie realized. Reuben was saying it all for her.

'I knew he wouldn't give up,' she said, as her mother stormed back to the house.

'The boy doesn't know what's good for him!' complained Mrs Diamond.

She saw Susie's grin. 'And neither do you, my girl. Oh, very well, if you two are determined to risk everything then the least I can do is show a little courage. Let's pray for a fine day.'

But as evening fell the clouds gathered. It rained all through the night, and in the morning they loaded the wagon in a downpour. Diamond Bright went in last, snorting at the puddles and pretending to be frightened. He looked wonderful, smart as paint in his rug and bandages, as if he came from a prosperous stable and not one about to be sold. To look at him no one would ever guess that he was their very last hope. When he pranced into the wagon Susie felt a great rush of affection and pride.

Flash stood in the rain, looking mournful, sensing that Reuben was about to leave him behind. Susie took pity on him. 'You can ride in the back with Diamond,' she told him. 'And you'd better be good.' Flash grinned at her and scuttled up the ramp.

But when they arrived at the event they almost thought it would be rained off. People were slopping around in puddles and mud, and horse boxes were stuck everywhere, being towed out by tractors. Their old wagon struggled and lurched. Susie got out and stood glumly watching as men tried to guide her mother across straw and wooden planking to a dry place. A girl walked by, wearing a leather Australian bushhat, the new horsey fashion. It was Naomi Fisher.

Naomi stopped. 'Don't tell me you're here,' she said sneeringly. 'Brought that Dobbin again, have you?'

'No,' said Susie. 'We've brought Diamond Bright.'

Naomi made a face. 'Everyone knows that horse is mad. Who's riding him? Not you. The only thing you're fit for is a pit pony. You and your know-all mother!'

Susie felt a flash of anger scorching her chest. If only she could tell Naomi that she was riding the horse. That would show her!

'Reuben Black is riding Diamond,' she said. 'You know him, the gypsy boy. He's a natural horseman. Not a nervous show-off like you!'

Naomi went red under her hat. 'I am not nervous! Anyway, why aren't you riding? You're supposed to be the amazing rider. You're the one who rode before they could walk. Don't tell me you're scared!'

Susie looked at Naomi's pretty face, twisted now by meanness and spite. She tried to think of some excuse for not riding, but suddenly she didn't want an excuse. Why should she lie to someone like Naomi Fisher? Why not tell her the truth? She tossed back the strands of wet red hair that stuck to her forehead.

'Yes,' she said. 'I am scared of Diamond Bright. He frightens me so I don't ride him well. And I'll tell you this, Naomi Fisher, the person who isn't scared of riding a horse they can't handle is a fool!'

She turned on her heel and marched to where her mother had at last parked the wagon. Reuben was letting the back down, whistling to himself between his teeth. He was excited, Susie realized. He knew he could ride Diamond Bright, and he wasn't afraid.

The horse was restlessly kicking the box, and Reuben went to lead him out. Rain or no rain, mud or no mud, Diamond had to be kept calm and happy.

He came down the ramp looking about him, his eyes alight with interest and intelligence, ears pricked, nostrils quivering to catch the unfamiliar scents of dozens of strange horses. As he neared the bottom of the ramp he stopped to take everything in, and Reuben let him stand for a moment or two and look around. He ran his hand down Diamond's gleaming chestnut neck.

'Better than staying at home, eh?' he asked him. 'Want to have a go, do you? Show them what you can do?'

Diamond whickered and dropped his nose to nuzzle the boy. Susie grinned and went back into the wagon to start getting the tack ready. Even with the rain, Diamond would do well today. She was sure of it.

At that moment Naomi Fisher came sneaking round the corner of the lorry. She held a water pistol in her hand and she looked furtive.

'What do you want?' asked Reuben, and she jumped. She was up to mischief and hadn't expected anyone to be standing on the ramp.

'Don't talk to me, you gypsy,' snapped Naomi. 'I can do what I like.'

'Not round here, you can't,' said Reuben. 'Get away from us.'

Flash, hearing the words 'get away', rose up from his place in the box and came to stand at Reuben's side. Naomi had heard that gypsies set their dogs on you. She saw tall, grey Flash and let out a piercing scream, shooting her water pistol wildly. 'Keep him off, keep him off!' she yelled.

The cold jet hit Diamond Bright full in the face. He reared up, losing his footing on the worn matting of the ramp, leaping and plunging in terror. Reuben clung to the horse's rope, at one moment swept off his feet, at the next dragged roughly against the metal edge of the wagon. Susie, running out, saw the sudden red spurt of blood.

'Let the horse go!' she yelled, but Reuben would die before he let Diamond race away into danger. He held on, as the horse slithered off the ramp and into the mud. Gradually Diamond calmed.

'I didn't mean it! I was only playing! He set the dog on me!' Naomi was whimpering with fright.

'You meant trouble,' snapped Susie. 'Go and get a doctor.'

Reuben was standing by the horse's head, smoothing Diamond's neck. His hand was shaking. A long cut gaped in his hair, oozing blood with a steady pulse. Blood was running into his eyes and Reuben kept ducking his head to wipe it away on his jacket. Flash whimpered unhappily, crouched down at his young master's feet.

'Let me have the horse,' said Susie, and eased the rope from Reuben's fingers.

'It were her fault,' he muttered. 'Her gave him a fright.' With that, he fainted at Susie's feet.

He was taken off to the St John's Ambulance tent, where a doctor stitched him up and sent him off to hospital for observation. He was conscious again, but still very groggy, and he kept insisting that he could ride. Even as they drove him away Susie and her mother could hear him saying, 'I'm not going to no ——— hospital! I've got the horse to ride!'

Mrs Diamond closed her eyes for a moment, struggling with tears. It was the end of all their dreams. At last she said, 'Poor Reuben. He's worked so hard for today. What a pity.'

'It was all Naomi Fisher's fault!' burst out Susie.

Her mother sighed. 'I never did like that family. I can't imagine why I let them foist that pony on us. Do you remember it, Susie?'

Susie nodded. A horrible pony. Just another of those that had made her hate riding. But she had sent the pony back to Naomi a great deal happier and better behaved than when it arrived, full of nerves and insecurity. Probably that was why Naomi hated her so.

A sudden squall of rain rushed across the field. Susie looked at her mother and saw that her cheeks were wet. Perhaps it was the rain. 'What shall we do now?' she asked.

Mrs Diamond tried to smile. 'Go home again, I suppose. We can spend the day turning out the loft and making piles of things to sell and things to throw away.' Her voice broke and she turned away quickly. They had all wanted so much from today.

A voice said, 'I'm going to ride Diamond Bright.'

Her mother turned back in amazement. 'What did you say, Susie?'

Susie swallowed. Had it been her? 'I just thought – I wanted – I want to ride Diamond. I know I can do it. I can, I've ridden in an event before.'

'But – aren't you frightened?'

Susie nodded. 'I'll probably fall off. But at least the ground's so squashy I won't get hurt. Please say I can.'

Mrs Diamond licked her lips. She was shaking with excitement. 'If only you could – I always wanted it to be you and Diamond Bright – and to be honest, Reuben's never any good at dressage. But it won't work. You're not used to each other. He won't go well.'

'He won't go at all if I don't ride him. I know the test backwards, and I can wear Reuben's kit.'

Her mother put a hand up to her head. 'I don't know. He's such a strong horse, and I should hate you to lose confidence again. He isn't like Doris. He might be the fastest horse here, he could do the cross-country in record time!'

'If the horse can do it, so can I,' said Susie bravely. 'Doris taught me to trust her and now I'm going to trust Diamond Bright.'

Mrs Diamond clenched and unclenched her fists. Suddenly she said, 'All right! But we've lost masses of time, suppose they won't take the entry?'

'Oh, everything's running late because of the rain,' Susie assured her. 'I'll dash over now and talk to them.'

'I'll do the horse,' shouted Mrs Diamond, hurrying away. And as they dashed in opposite directions a weak sun peeped out from behind the clouds, turning pools of water into shining mirrors of hope.

Diamond looked puzzled when Susie mounted. He

skittered sideways like an unbroken colt.

'Are you sure this is a good idea?' said Mrs Diamond nervously.

'Yes,' said Susie, whose own heart was bumping against her ribs. She sat down in the saddle, took up contact with the reins and moved Diamond off to the practice area. He trotted across with his graceful, prancing action, at each stride leaving the air with all four feet and seeming to hang there, suspended, for a frozen moment of time.

'Will you look at that horse?' someone said, and Susie straightened her back and lengthened her leg. They had to look good today.

As she practised, keeping an eye on the dressage arena to make sure she didn't miss her turn, she thought how much good Doris had done her. Things which she and Doris had struggled to achieve were easy with Diamond Bright. But the struggle meant she placed her aids exactly, and moved her weight just right, and picked up her mount's faults almost without thinking. What's more, all her life her mother had been training her. She had absorbed horsemanship without knowing that she did so, and now, with Diamond Bright, she needed every ounce. She knew, instinctively, that he was the best horse she had ever ridden, and the most difficult.

A flag, flapping on a tent, made him shy. He would be closer to that flag in the dressage arena, she thought, and concentrated on passing it smoothly and without fuss. But after ten minutes she could feel he was losing patience. He never liked doing anything for long. She pulled him up, gave him a loose rein, and let him graze.

'It's nearly your turn!' Her mother was screwing up the programme in an excess of nerves.

'It's OK. I'm ready. Could you wipe his mouth?'

Her mother mopped up the greenery as best she could. 'You shouldn't have let him graze,' she said anxiously. But it was better to have a calm horse with a green mouth than a wild horse with a clean one. They were waving to her to proceed. Susie gathered her reins and squeezed Diamond Bright into his best working trot.

She hardly remembered the test she had done on Doris, but she remembered every second with Diamond Bright. She concentrated so hard it made her head ache, and each time they approached the flag flapping on the tent she willed the horse to keep on past. He faulted once, badly, when he broke his extended trot for two canter strides. Susie brought him back to trot, gritting her teeth with the effort. Too many people let things go once they had made a mistake. She wasn't going to be one of them. She didn't need a brilliant test, just one that was good enough.

As they rode up for their final halt Susie could feel the horse buzzing with pent-up energy. She saluted the judges, tentatively letting Diamond walk away on a loose rein. He felt as if he might bolt off at any moment. No sooner had they left the arena and Susie had taken her first good deep breath than Diamond shied at the flag, bucked, and Susie flew off into the mud. She clung to the rein, gasping in surprise.

'It's all right, it's all right!' Her mother was dancing up and down beside her, splashing her more than ever. 'They can't fault you once you're out of the ring. Oh, Susie, that was brilliant! For a young horse too! I'm so proud of you, my darling.'

Susie struggled to her feet. There was even mud in her hair. Over her mother's shoulder she saw Naomi Fisher in the distance, pointing and laughing. Let her laugh, she thought. I have just ridden Diamond Bright.

But they had the cross-country to come. Susie felt the familiar cold stiffness come over her as she thought about it. Sometimes even Reuben couldn't hold Diamond, and he was far stronger than she. The memory of being run away with came back to her. Suppose that happened again?

'You've got the roads and tracks to take the fizz out of him,' said her mother, and gave an encouraging grin. 'Everyone's scared, you know, Susie.'

'You weren't.'

Mrs Diamond laughed. 'Oh yes, I was! Not as scared as you, perhaps. But you've lived almost all your life seeing how I was crippled by a riding accident. I didn't realize before but it's bound to have made you nervous. And I overhorsed you when you were little, and I didn't give you time. I'm just so glad I didn't put you off riding for ever.'

'It was Doris who cured me,' said Susie. 'Doris

and Reuben. And I'm going to say thank you with Diamond Bright.'

It hardly seemed any time before they found themselves waiting to start the cross-country. The rain was falling with gentle persistence, and all along the course were people in mackintoshes with umbrellas and wet dogs. Susie's mother had even brought Flash, because he was anxious about where Reuben had gone. She stood with one hand on Diamond's rein, the other holding Flash, and neither she nor Susie could think of anything to say.

They seemed to be waiting for eternity. Suddenly Susie saw a yellow mackintosh in the sea of people, and someone waving and calling. It was Mr Barnstaple.

'Susie! Hi, Susie! Best of luck!'

Her face cracked into a smile. It was good to see Mr Barnstaple. She waved and called back, 'Thanks,' and all of a sudden the starter was saying, 'Three – two – one – go!'

Diamond Bright plunged into a gallop. He was bred for this, born to it, and he was wasting no time. Susie let him run for a moment and then gathered him up. The first jump was upon them, but he flew it before she had time to think. She must plan ahead, she realized. On Diamond Bright there wasn't room for mistakes.

Two big plain fences sailed beneath them, almost without a check. But they were coming to the wood, a muddy, trappy place even on a fine day. The ground was like a skating rink. Diamond had to slow down and balance himself if they were to keep from coming to grief. Susie settled in the saddle, drawing him in, and for a moment he fought for his head. 'Steady,' she sang out, in a gentle, singsong voice, and he checked almost at once. He had known her voice from the first moments of his life. Then he saw the fence and checked again, exercising his natural intelligence. They popped into the wood, it was too dark to see, and Diamond broke into a trot. Thank goodness, there was the way, and she urged him on, telling him to trust her this time, she knew where they were going.

Once out in the open again she set him off in a good strong gallop. He was breathing smoothly and easily, eating up the yards between each fence. He began looking for the next obstacle, just as she did, and she knew he was thinking about what to do. On a fence with two drops, where he had to teeter on the edge of a little cliff and jump down and down again, Susie knew he was afraid. She urged him on with firm legs and a calm voice, and he took courage and went on. Reuben was right, she thought. You could hear a horse thinking.

The water jump was coming. The rain had swelled the stream to a vast pond and they had to ride for twenty strides through splashing water. There was no pond at home and Susie knew Diamond would be nervous. If Reuben was riding, the horse's faith would be in him, but she did not know if Diamond trusted her so completely. He might think she would do him harm, and take him into danger.

'It will be all right, Diamond,' she whispered to him. 'Just do what I say.'

He threw up his head as the sheet of water came into sight. Susie let him slow, and pushed him steadily on. But his head came up again, with a toss of the mane and a great snort of fear, and the horse slithered to a halt. The crowd let out a groan of disappointment, and above it, Susie could have sworn she heard someone laugh. Naomi Fisher, she thought.

'Come on, Diamond,' she said quietly. 'It's only water.'

The horse poked a tentative foot into the pond, and at that moment Susie clamped her legs on his sides. That, and Diamond's natural spirit, propelled him into the water in a great flurry of splashing, and they galloped, snorting, across the pond. In the last two strides Susie gathered him together and pushed him into his bridle, and he popped out like a cork from a shaken-up bottle, exploding over the fence a stride away almost without noticing. A great roar of applause went up and they galloped on, leaving a trail of spray and showering mud.

One refusal, thought Susie. Not bad for a first attempt. Suddenly the fences seemed small and the problems easily solved. We'll do a three-day event next time, she found herself thinking. This is fun.

When she cantered through the finish she saw Mr Barnstaple first. He was throwing his yellow oilskin hat into the air and shouting 'Yippee!' Mrs Diamond was trying to keep Flash out of the way of the horse, and was calling, 'Come here!' desperately, which made Flash strain at the end of his leash.

Susie pulled the horse up, and sat for a moment, getting her breath. Her heart was pounding like a hammer, and steam from Diamond Bright made it seem as if the world was shrouded in fog. Mrs Diamond was trying to come close to take the horse, but Flash was being too difficult. 'Tell him to get away,' called Susie. Her mother did, and was amazed as Flash walked to heel.

Susie giggled about it as she went to get weighed. She felt so full of lightness that giggling was likely to happen at any moment. Only the thought of poor Reuben lying in hospital stopped her collapsing on the floor and giggling for hours and hours. How odd it was that event days could be so miserable one minute and so wonderful the next, and sometimes the other way around. What a good thing every day wasn't like this.

When she came out of the tent she was surprised to see someone talking to her mother even as she led Diamond Bright in a steady, cooling circle. As she watched, another man came up, and a woman in a headscarf, and they all talked at once. Suddenly the saddle she held seemed to Susie to weigh like lead. There would be no next time with Diamond Bright. There would be no three-day event. This was what it was all about. The horse was to be sold.

Chapter Twelve

Reuben lay in his hospital bed, his face almost as white as the bandage round his head. Susie pulled out a chair and sat down. She felt so tired she thought she might almost slide off the chair and on to the floor.

'Where's your mum?' asked Reuben.

'Parking the car.'

It was late. Official visiting was over but the sister had said they could pop in for a moment or two. All the ward lights were out except for one or two above the beds, and they talked in low whispers, to avoid waking anyone.

'Sorry we're so late,' said Susie. 'We got held up. You see, I rode Diamond Bright.'

Reuben's eyes popped wide open. 'What?' he yelled, and the sister said, '*Shhhhh*', very loudly. 'What?' he said again in a hoarse whisper. 'You never had the bottle!'

'We had one refusal,' said Susie. 'At the water.'

'The water? Didn't settle him, did you? The water! Trust a girl.'

'If it hadn't been for the stop we'd have been

placed,' she went on. 'The showjumping was a doddle, they lowered the fences because of the wet. Everyone said he was marvellous for his first event. Anyway, if it had been you the water would have been OK but you'd have made a mess of the dressage. I'm streets better at that than you.'

Reuben didn't contradict her. His fingers reached out and began pleating the starched hospital sheet.

'I'm sorry it wasn't you,' said Susie.

He looked up and forced a smile. 'Well. Showed that Naomi girl, didn't it?'

Susie nodded. 'Yes.'

But she had to tell him. She simply had to. She took a deep breath and let it all out in a great rush. 'Reuben, I'm sorry but Diamond's gone. Sold. Three people were after him and they held a sort of auction and offered thousands of pounds, more than we ever expected. So we don't have to sell up after all. The man who bought him wouldn't even let us bring him home, he's some terribly rich businessman who sponsors riders and keeps an eye out for a likely horse. He says Diamond could compete at Badminton, or even the Olympics. He's still so young, you see. They don't often show such potential so soon. He took him straightaway.'

Reuben's black button eyes blinked at her. 'He's gone, you say? Gone?'

Susie nodded.

'But I never even said goodbye!'

The ward was quiet, with nothing but the rustle of people turning over in their sleep. A light rain spattered the window, and Susie thought how out of place Reuben looked here. He was too restless, too untidy. There were indoor people and there were outdoor people, and Reuben would always be an outdoor sort of person.

He sighed heavily. 'Like I always say,' he murmured. 'Good horses never stay. Keep the bad 'uns for ever.'

'Like Major,' said Susie. 'We can keep Major now.'

It seemed a terrible thought, a stable full of Majors and no Diamond Brights. But they still had Doris, she thought affectionately. Dear, reliable Doris. The sister waved at her from the end of the ward and Susie got up. Time to go. 'They say you can come out tomorrow,' she told Reuben. 'We'll come after lunch. OK?'

Reuben said nothing.

Susie woke the next morning with her heart like a balloon, filled with air one minute and lead the next. It was so wonderful that they could stay at home, and so terrible that they had lost Diamond Bright. The memory of yesterday kept confusing her, because it had been the best and the worst day of her life.

As soon as she had seen to the horses in the yard she went to see Doris in the field. All the gypsy ponies came up to the fence at once, but only Doris seemed to smile, and blink her large blue eyes. Susie petted her and tickled the groove under her lip, which always made Doris mumble in delight. There would never be another horse like Doris, she thought. There would never be another Diamond Bright.

A voice behind her said, 'Hello there, Susie! Going to come out riding with me? Of course, after yesterday, I might be beneath your touch.'

It was Mr Barnstaple, on Major. She turned and tried to smile. 'Of course you're not. I'll saddle Doris and come.'

'Great! I do like some company once in a while, and so does Major.'

Yes, thought Susie, going to fetch her tack. Major likes having a nice round rump in front of him so he can take a good big bite.

After Diamond Bright, Doris seemed terribly slow. What would it be like if I only ever had Doris to ride, Susie thought? It seemed disloyal to think of Doris as boring. But she was. And it was such a short time since she had decided that Doris was the best horse in the world.

A baby rabbit ran across the path in front of them, and Major snorted down his long nose.

'Your mother's feeling happier,' said Mr Barnstaple. He had taken her out for a drink the night before, to celebrate.

Susie nodded. 'She felt she was letting me down. But she's upset as well as happy. We're all going to miss Diamond Bright.'

'I don't think he was my sort of horse,' said Mr Barnstaple. 'Give me good old Major any day.'

Susie laughed. It seemed terribly funny that anyone would think Major was good. Oh well, it was a good thing Mr Barnstaple liked him.

After so much rain the day before the ground was soft as butter. They cantered along a grass verge, sending great clods of earth into the air. When they pulled up Mr Barnstaple patted Major's neck enthusiastically, and Susie moved Doris out of range of Major's teeth.

'There's something I've been meaning to ask you, Susie,' said Mr Barnstaple. 'You and your mother have been on your own for a long time now. I suppose you've got used to it.'

Susie nodded. 'Yes. It was awful to begin with, but not now. We still miss Dad terribly but it's not the same.'

'They say time is a great healer,' said Mr Barnstaple.

He was going red, thought Susie. Whatever was he trying to say?

'The thing is,' he went on, 'your mother and I – we've become very friendly of late. She's a remarkable woman. Courageous to a fault. Spirited, really. We were hoping – I was hoping – that you wouldn't mind if we got married.'

Susie felt as if she would fall off Doris in a dead faint. 'Married?'

He nodded. 'I've asked your mother and she says it's up to you. I love your mother very much, Susie, and you and I have always been friends. I should count it a great honour if you would welcome me into your life. So, what do you say?'

Her heart wasn't a balloon any more, it had turned into a rubber ball, bouncing wildly in her chest. Mr Barnstaple couldn't ever be her father. He couldn't take her father's place. And she was used to the way things were at home, the two of them, and Reuben, and the horses. Why couldn't they go on as they were?

'I'll have to think about it,' she said gruffly, and set Doris off in a brisk trot.

At home, her mother said nothing and neither did she. They went to get Reuben without speaking, and loaded him into the car as if he was a parcel. Even Reuben, who never spoke much himself, eventually noticed the silence.

'What's up?' he said at last. 'Someone died?'

Susie shook her head.

Mrs Diamond said desperately, 'I wish you'd say what you think, Susie! It's not so terrible, is it?'

Still Susie said nothing.

Reuben had instructions to stay in bed for a day or two, so Susie went up to his flat and sat in a chair next to him. He was trying to read a book on riding steeplechases. When Susie arrived he threw it down.

'Right fuss they make about that,' he said belligerently. 'I could do that. Give me a chance and I'd do it easy.'

Susie picked up the book and glanced at it. 'Yes. You probably could. My mother knows a man who trains steeplechasers.'

'Your mum knows everyone,' said Reuben. 'Yatter, yatter, yatter, that's all her sort do. Yatter, yatter, yatter, about horses.'

Susie looked at him from under her lashes. 'You still upset about Diamond?' she asked.

Reuben shrugged. 'Never know. Might come

back. When no one else can ride him. Has Danny come?'

She shook her head. 'What for?'

'Doris. You don't need Doris no more.'

Susie gaped at him, her eyes wide with horror. Not need Doris? Doris to go? Everything was going, Diamond Bright, her mother, and now this! Everything had been so wonderful yesterday and now everything was lost. She ran down the stairs and out into the yard, racing across the slippery cobbles to the field gate. The ponies were gone. Where Doris had stood this morning, mumbling the grass and blinking, was now an empty space.

'Doris!' she yelled, hopelessly. 'Doris!' And there was an answering whinny from the lane.

She saw Doris first, although Danny had all the ponies. He was standing by the hedge, waiting for her.

'Reuben said you was ready,' he muttered as she raced up.

'I'm not! I'm not ready at all! Oh, Doris!' She put her arms around the mare and buried her face in her thick neck.

'Figured you'd be upset, saying goodbye.' Danny hopped from one foot to the other. 'Left you a present, I did. Some rabbits.'

'Rabbits?' Susie lifted her head.

'Good eating, rabbit. Hung on the fence they was.'

Susie thought about eating rabbit and felt ill. 'Thank you,' she said weakly.

But Danny still seemed embarrassed. 'Want me to leave her, do you?'

Susie stroked Doris's big flat face. Dear Doris. Kind Doris. What would the days be like without Doris and her calm good sense? Then she remembered this morning with Mr Barnstaple. For a brief, disloyal moment she had thought Doris ordinary and dull. It was like when she was little, she thought suddenly, with Topic and Dandelion, and all the other ponies she had loved and learned from. You had to know when it was time to move on, to let the ponies go to someone who really needed them. It wasn't fair to keep good ponies just as ornaments in a field. They deserved better than that. Susie felt tears threatening again. Much as she loved her, it was as Reuben said. She didn't need Doris any more.

'You take her,' she said huskily to Danny. 'It's OK. I just wanted to say goodbye.'

She stood in the lane and watched the horses walk away, bunched together by the ropes in Danny's hand. Doris glanced back, once, and Susie raised her arm in farewell. She wasn't the first person Doris had helped and she wouldn't be the last. A horse like that never got tired of being generous.

When she got back to the yard she found Reuben out of bed, sweeping up. He kept on, even though she was watching him. He had put fresh straw in some of the boxes, as if he expected new horses to appear at any moment.

'We haven't anything coming,' Susie told him. 'All the liveries have gone, except Major. We've hardly anything here now.'

'Your mum can't help getting horses,' said Reuben calmly. 'Best to be prepared.'

'She's going to marry Mr Barnstaple,' said Susie.

Reuben sniffed. 'Dare say she is. She's pretty. Like you.'

'Like me?' Susie coloured to the roots of her hair.

'Yeah.' Reuben scowled at her. 'But don't you go getting vain. All new clothes and stuff you'll have, when your ma gets wed. Bet he's got money.'

Susie thought about it. New clothes. No more misery on own-clothes day at school, when everyone else had something trendy and she felt a freak. And Mr Barnstaple wasn't so bad. She liked him a lot, really. But the horses, the horses! She looked at the empty boxes and wondered how she could ever have wanted a life without them.

'You ought to go and lie down,' she told Reuben.

Mr Barnstaple came to tea that afternoon. He was very polite and Mrs Diamond fussed around him, pink faced and uncomfortable. They both kept looking at Susie. As her mother splashed tea on the table and got in a state because she'd made the cake soggy, Susie said, 'I think it's a very good idea for you to get married. Congratulations.'

'Susie!' Her mother splashed more tea, ruining the cake altogether.

'Susie!' Mr Barnstaple reached out and squeezed her hand, beaming all over his kind, sensible face.

Susie almost wished she hadn't said anything, they were making such a fuss. A wagon was pulling into the yard. She got up and went to the window. 'I bet they've come to the wrong stables,' she said.

'They can't be here already,' said her mother, getting to her feet. 'It's only half past five.'

'Forget about tea,' said Mr Barnstaple. 'Come on, Susie. Take a look at this.'

The three of them went out to the yard, and in a second Reuben and Flash joined them. 'I thought you were supposed to be in bed,' said Mrs Diamond, but Reuben said nothing. He was never where he was supposed to be.

'OK to get him out?' said the wagon driver, and they all nodded. The ramp was let down.

Out stepped a horse. Coal black but for a spatter of white across his rump, like snowflakes on soot, he put his head up and sniffed the air. Then he picked his way down the ramp, at the last moment taking fright and skittering sideways.

'Steady, lad. Steady,' said the driver. 'He's young yet. Bit on the wild side, too. Handle that sort, can you?'

'Some of us can,' said Mrs Diamond. 'What do you think, Susie? Reuben? He's called Dark Morning.'

'Wow,' said Susie.

But Reuben only sniffed. 'Make something of him, I suppose,' he muttered. 'Take some riding. Good thing you got me, that's what I say.'

The others exchanged laughing glances. 'We do say, Reuben,' said Mrs Diamond. 'It's what we all say.'